Caroline Plaisted worked in publishing for fourteen years before the birth of the first of her two children. Since then she has written more than twenty books and now also edits an art magazine. She lives in Kent.

Also available by Caroline Plaisted from Piccadilly:
Reality Bites Back!
Re-inventing Mum

love

a story of first love on the internet

Caroline Plaisted

Piccadilly Press • London

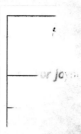

First published in Great Britain in 2001
by Piccadilly Press Ltd.,
5 Castle Road, London NW1 8PR

A catalogue record for this book is available from
the British Library

ISBNs: 1 85340 628 7 (trade paperback)
1 85340 623 6 (hardback)

1 3 5 7 9 10 8 6 4 2

Printed and bound in Great Britain by Bookmarque Ltd.

Cover design by Paul Fielding Design Ltd.
Set in 10.75pt Gill Sans and Courier 10pt

Chapter 1

frt?
(Free to talk?)

You can't be serious? S

I am! My mum said she saw her calmly step out of her knickers and put them in her bag. C

At the bus stop? Never. S

She did, I tell you! Mum said she couldn't believe it. Says she'll never be able to look her in the eye at a parent-teacher meeting again! C

Don't think I will at the next lesson either. S

You going to do your Physics stuff tonight? C

'Samantha! Hi! I'm home! Samantha, darling? Where are you?' It was Mum!

Gotta go! My mum's back. cya 2morrow. S

Bibi. C

I left the chatroom and clicked on to one of my bookmarked websites. The last thing I needed was my mum catching me chatting to my mate Claudia on the net. I have to admit to feeling just a little bit guilty about it – I'd spent nearly the last hour talking to Claudia and Debs on-line, when I really should have been doing my Physics.

Claudia and Debs are two of my best mates. Claudia's parents are Italian and they've got this restaurant. They all live in a flat above it so Claudia gets to eat in a restaurant every day of her life! And she's fluent in Italian too – as well as being gorgeous enough to be a model. Claudia's brilliant at Art and Textiles and she wants to go to Art college.

Debs on the other hand is into science – in fact she wants to be a doctor like her aunt. Only thing is, her aunt is a pathologist and Debs reckons that she wants to work with live bodies not dead ones. Debs is great. I suppose if I had to choose one girl out of my friends that I would confide in most it would be her.

'Samantha?' There was a gentle knock on my bedroom door. Then the door was pushed wider open. 'Samantha? Are you OK?'

6

'Oh, hi, Mum. How you doing?' I scrolled down the screen as if I was searching for something.

'I'm OK, love, how about you? See you've made a head start on your homework, then. What is it tonight?'

'Erm, Physics.' I could feel my cheeks burning as I fibbed. Any minute now my mum would realise that I didn't even have any books out. 'I'm looking for some stuff that Miss Maddox said would be on the Royal Institute website. Hey!' I remembered Claudia's last bit of juicy goss. 'You'll never guess! You remember Mrs Dixon our Geography teacher? Well, Claudia says her mum saw her at the bus stop and her knickers fell down! In front of everyone! Can you imagine?'

'That can't be true, Samantha. Really it can't.' Mum sat down on my bed, eased off her smart new shoes and rubbed the backs of her heels. 'When's she meant to have seen this, then?'

'The other night, outside Claudia's parents' restaurant. She said she was cool as a cucumber and just stepped out of them.' I got the giggles just thinking about it. I laughed so much that Mum started to join in. 'Claudia's mum says she doesn't think she'll be able to talk to her at the next parents' evening.'

'I can understand why. Oh, poor woman. If it's true, Mrs Dixon must have been so embarrassed. Makes you wonder how it happened though, doesn't it? Dear, dear,' Mum

7

laughed and shook her head, then rubbed her heels again. 'Nothing as entertaining as that happened in court today, I can tell you.'

My mum (she's called Laura) is a lawyer. She's dead smart and she specialises in family law – you know, divorce and children's welfare, that sort of thing. Today she'd spent the day in court so she was looking even smarter than usual. Dressed from head to foot in black in a sharp trouser suit that she'd recently bought and some simply gorgeous shoes that I'd forced her to buy last weekend.

Mum glanced at her watch. 'Suppose I'd better get organised with some supper.' She pulled herself up to her feet and took her jacket off. 'Supper at about seven thirty, Samantha?'

'Sure, I'll just get on with this stuff.'

I spent the next hour or so searching the net and finding the material about Physics that I needed for my GCSE coursework. I don't want to sound like a swot or anything but I think school and stuff is generally pretty cool. Now that may be because the school I go to is the business. It's all girls, which some people may think is a bit of a drag, but there is a boys' school with some fit lads fairly close to it. I've explained about two of the girls who are my friends already. The other special one's Butter – her real name is Flora but we all call her Butter because of the margarine – geddit?

Butter comes from this enormous family. She's got four brothers and a baby sister who's only six. Can you imagine four brothers? They're all a bit geeky though, if you ask me. But I wouldn't tell Butter that. Butter's got this short blonde hair (natch) and she's absolutely hooked on sport. She's in our school cricket team. She's so good, Mrs Sutton our Sports teacher is thinking of putting her forward for the national team this year.

Anyway, I typed up the material that I'd got off the net and started closing down my PC. The little mailbox icon flashed on the screen.

'Samantha! Supper's ready in five minutes!' Mum called up the stairs, delicious smells wafting up ahead of her words.

'Down in a sec!' I had to check out my mail first, didn't I?

From: debs@doobopdaloola.com
To: sam@newshoes.com

Sam
Claudia says Mrs Dixon lost her knickers
outside the restaurant the other night!
Straight! Gran says we should call her
Droopy Drawers from now on.
cya, Debs

I could almost feel sorry for Mrs Dixon because if Claudia

and her mum had anything to do with it, the whole world would know about her drastic elastic before long. But now it was time for some scoff.

Mum and I nearly always eat on our own. My dad isn't around much during the week because he usually works away from home. Dad (his name's Paul) is an IT systems analyst. He's always off working on new programs for these big companies all over the country. Sometimes he even does it abroad. So he does a lot of travelling and, really, he's away far more than he's at home during the week. But when he does come home he's always got the latest software gimmicks to load on to our PCs. It's pretty cool really.

Now my mum's job is really demanding. I mean, she's never home before six o'clock and some evenings she does more work once we've eaten. Some of my friends think it's weird that my mum and dad work so much and don't have much free time during the week. To be honest it doesn't really bother me. I suppose I'm just used to it and get on with my own thing and no one bothers me.

Most weekends though we go to the club. It's one of the perks of Dad's job: family membership to the local private health club. Mum likes it because of the steam rooms and sunbeds. Dad plays squash (there's always a neighbour who wants to play with him). I like to swim (the pool is gorgeously warm and isn't full of der-brains trying to bomb you all the time like at the other pool in town) and Mum and I play tennis nearly every week – although I'm not sure that Mum plays because she enjoys it. I think it's more because she spends the time with me and I enjoy it.

Mum and I ate supper in the kitchen and Mum told me all about the case she'd been representing in court that day. It was a kind of sad but happy one about these two little kids who were orphans but were about to be formally adopted by their aunt and uncle. Sometimes Mum tells me a bit about her cases – you know, families being broken up, with brothers and sisters getting separated between parents. Actually, I don't think she tells me anything like what really goes on. Partly because she's not allowed to and also because some of the stuff is just so sad. When she's working in the evening you can see this great furrow between her eyebrows. Sometimes you can hear her muttering stuff under her breath and shaking her head in disbelief that people can be so awful to each other.

This night she said, 'That's enough about my work today. What did you find out from the Royal Institute?'

So I told Mum all about the stuff our Physics teacher wanted us to do. Then Mum mentioned that Dad hoped to be home the next day.

'Come on,' she said. 'Let's load up the dishwasher. I've got some paperwork to read and then I'm going to put my feet up and watch the telly. How about you?'

'I've got a little bit more work to do and then I think I might join you on the sofa.'

Forty-five minutes later I'd had enough of my coursework. I was just about to switch off my PC but I couldn't resist one last peep into the chatroom the girls and I have discovered. I logged on.

There were two girls whose names I didn't recognise having a debate about some corny rock band. I flipped on to the message board. Lots of the messages had been there yesterday but there was one that caught my eye.

```
Boy, 17, seeks rescuer from study boredom.
Must like animals and find younger brothers
irritating. Anyone out there? Please send
me a message!
```

Hmmm. Seventeen. What was any decent seventeen-year-old boy doing leaving messages on a chatroom notice-board? I mean, he must be some sort of geek, mustn't he? Or he wouldn't need to find friends that way, would he? Obviously a sad case. I logged off, switched off the light and went down to watch the telly with Mum.

Later that night, after the telly, a bath and a good read, I flicked off the light and wondered about 'Boy, 17'. I mean, he was obviously a nerd. But then I'd been into the chatroom and read his message, hadn't I? So didn't that make me a sad case too? Help!

Chapter 2

ne1 there?
(Anyone there?)

It was Art after break the next day. I can't pretend that Art is my best subject but I really enjoy it. I mean you can relax a bit in Art and enjoy slopping the paint together. Mrs Thomas, our teacher, plays music while we work. She says it's to get us in the mood and she chooses different types of music depending on what project we're working on. Sometimes it might be Madonna, other times jazz or classical stuff. We spent some time working on religious paintings – you know, icons and rood-screens, that sort of thing – and Mrs Thomas played us Mozart's Requiem. It really got us in the mood.

Anyway, this day, we were trying to paint what Mrs Thomas called 'hot paintings'. We had to try to paint thinking Africa and Morocco, so we had this amazing African dance music we were working to. I was busy swirling some spicy blue tones together for my piece, staring out of the window as I did it. Thinking about 'Boy, 17'.

What could he be like? I mean, why wasn't he able to chat

to his own friends like I did? Surely they could help to rescue him from his studying? Unless, of course, he didn't have any friends. Perhaps that was it! Perhaps he was just some kind of sad bloke who couldn't make friends and had to rely on chatrooms in order to have anyone in his life. There were a couple of girls like that at school – you know, the ones who never join in with anything and sit quietly in the corner of the classroom by the door. They never take part in class discussions, seem to miss most school trips and never, ever come to school discos. But they always, always do their homework on time and have exactly the right school uniform on. The more I thought about it, the more I reckoned 'Boy, 17' was the boy version of one of these girls.

'Penny for them, Samantha?' Mrs Thomas waved her hand in front of my face.

I came to with a start and almost dropped my paintbrush full of hot turqoise into the mixing tray.

'Sorry?'

'Penny for them – your thoughts. Penny for your thoughts, Samantha?'

'Oh, sorry, Mrs Thomas. I was just wondering what the colour of the African sky is really like,' I lied, feeling my cheeks start to flush scarlet.

'Well it looks like you've got a good colour to start with there, Samantha. I'll look forward to seeing what you're doing with it in a minute.' She wandered over to Butter, who was already creating a huge Matisse-like picture of orange and yellow.

My paper was still sparkling white – I hadn't even done any pencil outlines. My thoughts were about 'Boy, 17' and I didn't know why I was wasting my time wondering about a geek like him. I felt irritated and cross with myself as I started painting.

At break, Butter was in a foul mood. She was furious because she'd been caught by Mr Simpson (he's the deputy head) using her mobile phone between lessons.

'He's only gone and confiscated my phone! I mean, what right's he got to do that? How dare he? I was only ringing my brother anyway to find out what the latest test scores are. I mean, it's not as if I was ringing *during* the lesson – just between. I ask you!'

'Well, there is the rule,' Debs said.

Butter glared at her. 'What?'

'The rule,' Debs said it again. 'That says we aren't allowed to have our phones switched on at school.'

'Huh!' Butter carried on glaring, this time at her feet which she started to kick against the locker she had been leaning on. 'That.' Her cheeks were glowing red.

'Yeah, that,' Claudia laughed. 'You moron! Fancy phoning

during school! I mean, it's not as if Mr Simpson doesn't go on and on about mobile phones, is it?'

Butter's face was burning — I reckoned with embarrassment as well as anger. We all know that we can take phones to school, just as long as we don't use them during school hours. 'OK, OK! Don't keep on at me about it!'

'So,' I tried to pacify Butter. 'When's he going to give you the phone back, then?'

Butter flicked her hair behind her ear. 'Said he'd keep it in the office until the end of the day. I've got to collect it after the last period and then the toerag has said I've got to hand the phone into the office every morning for the next week.'

'Well, it could be worse,' Claudia said soothingly.

'It could? I don't see how.' It was typical of Butter to overreact like this.

'Yes — I mean, he could have taken away your phone completely, couldn't he?'

'Well he has, hasn't he? I mean, I don't think I can spot it about me now, can I?' She made exaggerated gestures, pretending to look for her phone in all her pockets and her bag.

Debs giggled. 'Oh Butter! Don't be so daft! So, you've lost your mobile for the rest of the day. Big deal! You were hardly likely to get many phone calls before four o'clock, were you?'

'Well, I could have got some text messages!' Butter snorted. And then she started to laugh at herself too. She was being a bit moronic. 'Who knows who wants to get hold of me any time of day! Brad Pitt . . . Leonardo . . .'

'Oh yeah – and the boy down at the chip shop who says he's Elvis!' Claudia said and we all giggled.

That was when the bell went.

'Double Maths . . .' I groaned. 'Yum, yum.'

We all trooped off in the direction of Mr Walker's square roots.

Butter immediately hunched her coat over her shoulders and started to do her impression of our Maths teacher. Mr Walker was totally disgusting to look at and we were all convinced that he was probably one of the characters from a Steven King novel. But he was seriously good at teaching Maths. No one ever failed in his class – a fact that we all reluctantly acknowledged.

'Get out of here!' Claudia pretended to bash Butter over the head with her arm.

'Now then, now then, girls, settle down. Eyes up!' Butter pointed her finger at us all, exactly the same way that Mr Walker did at the beginning of every lesson. We all collapsed with laughter again as we fumbled our way along the corridor to A Block. But before we got to the block doors, we suddenly heard a voice behind us.

'Now then, now then, girls, settle down! Let's get along to the class please!'

It *was* Mr Walker! He was right behind us! By this time we were hysterical. Double Maths, here we were . . .

'See you later, Sam!' Debs banged on the bus window and waved before she set off down the road to home where she lived with her parents and gran. Debs's gran came from the West Indies and she was always promising Debs that one day she's going to take her back there to introduce her to all her family. I'd already told Debs that I was going with them in her suitcase! As usual, I stayed on the bus. It was Friday and Fridays always meant one thing: piano lesson at Mrs Jay's.

Mrs Jay lives on her own in quite a big Victorian terraced house. Fortunately, her house is on the way home to mine so, although going to her on a Friday was a bit of a drag, it wasn't that bad. At least I didn't have hours of travelling to get there and back. When she was young, Mrs Jay was a star pupil at the Royal Academy of Music – or so she says. But actually, I think she's telling the truth. She was expected to become a star concert pianist and travel the world but then tragedy struck. Apparently her dad died and her mum expected her to return home immediately and look after her. Give up her career and stuff. It's awful. I can't imagine giving up all my friends, all that freedom of living away from your parents. All that travelling around the world! But Mrs Jay talks about it as if that was exactly what she expected to have to do. As if it was obvious that she would return home and look after her mother. Giving kids like me piano lessons instead of listening to the sound of applause ringing in her ears. Dead sad. Even sadder though, was that Mrs Jay never got back to being a concert pianist. She married but then her husband upped and died on her and left her alone with her mother again. Mrs Jay's mum died a couple of years ago. And now Mrs Jay lives there on her own. And she's still teaching.

As I opened the gate to Mrs Jay's house, for some weird reason I thought about 'Boy, 17' again. I wondered if he played the piano, or some other instrument?

'That's right, Samantha, move with the music, dear! Feel it from the tips of your fingers, up your arms and then up your neck until it makes the hair on your head tingle with the excitement!' Mrs Jay always got really involved with the lesson. When I was a kid, I used to think it was all just a bit of a joke. All that stuff about tingling, you know? But now I really like Mrs Jay. I kind of love the way that she really gets into the music and she loses all sense of everything else in the room – except me, of course! And the more I play the piano, the more I realise what she's talking about. I mean, you really can get lost in the music and forget all about your schoolwork and everything else.

I finished the piece and Mrs Jay started to scribble away in my practice book. She was putting down all the things she wanted me to practise between now and my next lesson.

'There, Samantha.' She handed my book to me with a great beaming smile and put her pen in her pocket.

'Thanks, Mrs Jay.' I started to gather all my sheet music and things into my music case and then I stood up.

Mrs Jay padded her way across the room and led the way downstairs with me following her. At the bottom of the stairs I grabbed my jacket and my school bag and opened the door. 'Thanks, Mrs Jay. I'll see you next week, then,' I called behind me as I left.

'Goodbye, Samantha, dear. Have a lovely weekend,' Mrs Jay waved, peering from behind the already half closed door.

'Yes – and you!' I shut the gate behind me. ('Always such a good girl,' I could hear Mrs Jay saying to my mum like she always did at the last lesson of every term that Mum came to so that she could keep up with my progress.)

I switched on my phone as I walked towards the bus stop. I had a text message from Debs:

```
ru3 2nite? spk
   2u l8r
```

There was another almost identical message from Butter as well. 'spk 2u l8r' was our own code for getting on to the net to chat and I sent them both the same message back:

gr8 thx

Then the bus arrived at my stop and I hopped on. It was the weekend. Gr8!

Dad was home when I got there.

'Hello, chicken! How are you?' He gave me a great bear hug. 'How was Mrs Jay today? Mum tells me that you're doing really well with your sonata. Come on into the kitchen. We're cooking supper – you must be starving, aren't you?' Dad disappeared down the hall into the kitchen. It was typical of him not to give me a chance to reply to any of his questions. It's not that he isn't interested in finding out about people. It's just that he talks really quickly and is always on the move. Mum says he never really winds down from the week until Sundays, when he tends to slob out on the sofa with a pile of newspapers on top of him. Quite often, he's asleep underneath them too.

In the kitchen, Mum was busy cutting and slicing

22

vegetables while Dad was oiling a wok.

'Hello, Samantha. Good day?' Mum was beaming. She was never miserable when Dad was away during the week, but you could tell straight away how happy she was to have him home.

'Fine, thanks. That lot looks good.'

'Yes,' Dad said, pinching a piece of pepper from Mum's chopping board and popping it in his mouth. Still munching, he said, 'I thought I'd cook a Chinese dish I saw that bloke cook on the telly the other day. Hungry? I'm starving and I thought we might as well eat now that you're here.'

'OK. I'll just pop upstairs and change. Call me when it's ready, will you?'

'Of course, darling, but it's a stir-fry so don't take long.' Mum smiled and Dad started to mix up various liquids in a bowl. He was in his element.

In my room, my gorgeous cat Charly was curled up asleep at the end of my bed. As usual, she'd wedged herself between the bookcase at the foot of the bed and the wall. As I switched the light on, she twitched an ear at me and let out a purr of greeting.

Gently, I stroked her shiny black fur. I don't think there is another cat in the world quite as beautiful as Charly.

I threw off my school uniform and turned the screen of

my PC on. I looked at my watch and wondered if there was enough time to have a chat with my friends.

'Samantha!' It was Dad calling up the stairs. 'Supper's ready!' I guessed the girls would have to wait.

Over supper, Dad told us about what he'd been doing that week. Something to do with a big firm in Birmingham setting up a new customer services system. I'm sure it was interesting but . . . well, I wasn't really in the mood. Anyway, I had 'Boy, 17' to think about. I mean, maybe he was talking to someone on-line right now!

In between gabbling on, Dad darted questions to Mum and me about what we'd been doing and then gave us a fraction of a second to answer. After about half an hour of this, Mum suddenly butted in and said to Dad, with a smile on her face, 'For goodness sake, Paul, calm down a bit! Take a breather and think about what you'd like to have for pudding. Samantha, what would you like? There's ice cream or fruit — or both,' she said, looking directly at me with a smile.

'Both, please!'

Mum and Dad laughed and we all cleared the table before I dished out three rather generous helpings of Häagen Dazs.

'Mum? Do you mind if I take mine upstairs? I've got some stuff to do.' Like 'Boy, 17', I thought.

'Of course, darling.' Mum smiled.

'You're a good girl, Samantha. You work hard. The only way to get anywhere these days is to work hard.' Dad put his arm around me, giving me a congratulatory hug. If only he knew!

'See you later, then,' I waved my spoon as I left the kitchen. Halfway up the stairs I heard Mum giggle and I turned round. Mum and Dad were smooching with each other. Parents are just disgusting sometimes.

Once I was safely upstairs with Charly I went into the chatroom and announced myself. Looking at my watch, I was expecting to find some of the girls there already chatting. After a couple of seconds though, there was no response. So I tried again.

Hi! It's Sam!

The cursor blinked for a while and then someone cruised in.

Hi, Sam! I'm Dan, fancy a chat?

Now this wasn't what I was expecting at all! I was expecting one of the girls. Not someone called Dan. For a fraction of a second I wasn't sure what to do.

Sorry, Dan. I'm looking for my friends.

> Can't you chat with me while you're
> waiting? I need someone to rescue me from
> my revision tonight.

Did he say revision? He needed rescuing from revision? That sounded like 'Boy, 17'. I could feel myself going all wobbly. I needed a mouthful of ice cream to calm my nerves.

OK then. But I'll have to go as soon as my friends get here.

I wrote it without thinking first. It was a good job he couldn't see me blushing. I felt such a twit! I must have sounded like some kind of Brownie or something.

> OK. I won't keep you from your pals. So
> tell me, Sam, how are you? Where are you?
> And how old are you?

The cursor blinked for a second.

> And are you a girl-Sam or a boy-Sam?

Now I wasn't born yesterday. I know that you have to be a bit careful about what you give away to people when you're on-line. I mean, we've all read in the papers about those weirdos out there, haven't we? You know, all those dirty old men who try and chat to young kids.

Well, tell me about you first, Dan. How old are you and where are you?

OK. I'll go first. I'm 17 and I live in the country. What about you?

So he was 'Boy, 17'! But surely he couldn't be *the* 'Boy, 17'? After all, there must be loads of seventeen-year-olds out there surfing the net . . .

Chapter 3

brb
(Be right back)

My fingers froze on the keyboard. Supposing it was him, though? You know, 'Boy, 17'. For a second, I couldn't think of anything to say.

> Sam? You still there?

I had to say something, didn't I?

Yes.

The cursor blinked at me, begging me to say something to 'Boy, 17'.

So, are you waiting to talk to your friends too?

> No. I've been revising and I'm bored. I
> wanted someone to cheer me up.

What are you revising, then?

Chemistry, Physics, Biology. All that
stuff. How about you? You doing exams?

**Yes. GCSEs. Your subjects and all the usual
others as well.**

So are you 15 then, Sam?

I thought I must have blown it. I mean, if he was seventeen,
he probably wouldn't want to talk to a fifteen-year old, would
he? The cursor was blinking at me again, asking for a
response.

Sam? Have you gone?

I wanted to answer him in case he went away. I really don't
know why, but I wanted to find out more about him.

Sam?

Sorry, I'm here.

Good. Thought you'd gone away. You must be
taking GCSEs next summer, then. I'm doing
my A levels next year and then I'm off to
university. At least I hope I am.

So, what did you say your name was?

It's Dan. Where do you live, Sam?

Huh. He wasn't going to get it out of me that easily.

London.

That was nice and vague.

How about you?

We could both ask, couldn't we?

In the Midlands. Quite a rural place. Not in the city like you. Do you like living in the city, then?

He said it as if it was something I had a choice about.

Course I do. It's the only place I've ever lived. How about you? Do you like living in your rural place?

Yes. But I've never lived anywhere else. Never lived in a city. In fact, I've only been to London once.

When was that?

Couple of years ago. We came on a school trip to the theatre.

I love the theatre and was always trying to persuade my mum and dad to take me at the weekends. Sometimes I actually managed it.

What did you see? At the theatre?

We went to the Royal National Theatre. Saw The Cherry Orchard for GCSE. It was really good.

I saw that! It was fantastic. Helen Mirren was in it. She was brilliant.

Is she the woman who does all the telly plays?

Well he obviously wasn't that big on culture, was he?

Yes. I can't believe that you saw the same play.

Small world, really. So, what are you up to this weekend?

Was this a trick question from a weirdo? Or was this just 'Dan, 17' asking what I was up to for the weekend?

Nothing much. Hanging around with my friends, studying. How about you?

> Pretty much the same. Only you can't
> really hang around with your mates much
> round here. Everyone lives too far away.
> But my mum's lending me her car to go over
> to see my mate Will tomorrow evening.

He could drive! Wicked. 'Dan, 17' was beginning to sound rather cool.

When did you pass your test?

PLINK! That was the call sign for one of the girls.

That's my friends, I think. Sorry, Dan. I've got to go.

This time there was a silence from his end. The cursor blinked at me for a second or two before there was any response.

> Never mind. But I was enjoying our chat.
> Do you think you might chat again another
> night, Sam?

Well, well.

Might do.

There was no point in looking too keen. After all, he might

think I was so sad that I hadn't got anything better to do than just sit waiting to chat to boys like him. As if!

Perhaps another night, Dan. Maybe we'll chat again.

`OK then. Maybe we will. Bye`

Bye

Then he was gone. There was the PLINK! noise again. It was Butter by the look of it (we'd all given ourselves signs that only we knew – you know, to keep it private), and Debs. There was another PLINK! This time it was Claudia.

They'd probably already started chatting. Before I joined in, I thought for a minute about my chat with Dan. Perhaps I'd been too cool. I mean, perhaps I hadn't sounded that keen about chatting to him again. I might have put him off, mightn't I? He probably thought I wasn't interested. And I was. I did want to chat to him again. He sounded nice. Cool. Oh, stuff! He was probably really fit and I'd gone and completely blown it. Oh, well . . . it was too late now. Dan had gone.

I went back into the main chat area and logged on. The girls pounced straight away. Debs butted in first – I could tell because we all identified ourselves by giving our initials at the end of the chat.

WHERE'VE YOU BEEN, SAM? D

Busy. What's up? S

We're talking about Mrs Dixon's knickers. B

Still? S

Course! C

OK. WHAT U BEEN UP TO, SAM? D

**Not much. Supper. Music lesson. Pretty much
the same as you lot. What u up to tomorrow? S**

And we chatted like that for at least another half-hour,
catching up on nothing mostly. You know what it's like. You
say goodbye to your friends at school and then you chat
away like crazy on the net when you get home. It's great.
Your mum and dad think you're busy doing your homework
when you're actually chatting to your mates for at least some
of the time. OK, some nights it's most of the time. Still, as
Butter's dad said when he opened a huge phone bill one day,
he'd rather we were chatting via the net because it was
cheaper than using the phone. So that's when we really
started using the chatroom so much.

Charly curled her gorgeous self up on my lap as I tapped
away on the keyboard. The only thing that wasn't so good
about using the chatroom was that you couldn't hear each

other laughing. After we finished finding out about what we were all up to for the weekend, and then finding out what the others had seen on 'Top of the Pops' while I was having supper with Mum and Dad, we signed off.

I flicked the button on my screen and then took Charly and lay down on my bed with her. I thought about Dan. Was he real or just someone pretending to be him? He sounded nice. He sounded interesting. In the end, I decided that if he was just pretending, then it was a funny thing to pretend about – going to the theatre. After a while I got into bed but, irritatingly, instead of being able to sleep I kept wondering if 'Boy, 17' would chat again another night, like he said. And whether he'd find out if I was a girl at some stage. Why did this boy keep preying on my mind?

On Saturday mornings Mum and Dad (if he was around) always went to the supermarket to do the shopping. Frankly, I can't stand going. It's just so boring, so I try to get out of it. I make the most of having a nice long lie-in and then, if I'm feeling like it, I might spend some time practising the piano. On this particular Saturday, that's exactly what I did. Charly curled herself up on the sofa while I practised this really cool new piece Mrs Jay had given me to start learning for my next piano exam. It was by an American composer, and really modern. I'd never played anything like it before.

There I was, twiddling away, when Mum and Dad came back. Dad popped his head around the door.

'We're just going to put the shopping away and then have some coffee before we go off to the club. So we'll be off in about twenty minutes, love, is that OK?'

'Sure,' I called over my shoulder as I carried on trying to tackle the music. 'Can I have a coffee too? I'll be finished in a minute.'

It was more or less the same routine every Saturday and this one was no exception. After coffee, we went off to the club. Dad played squash and Mum and I bashed it out on the tennis court before we met him again in the café for lunch. I think lunch was one of Dad's treats to us for having been away all week. We carried on with the bits and pieces of conversations we started the night before over supper. Mum tried to persuade me to go on a tennis camp during the summer holiday but I wasn't sure that I wanted to go. Not on my own anyway. None of my friends would be going. In the end, I said I'd think about it, mostly to make her stop going on about it. And then I went for a swim while Mum went on a sunbed (no matter how many times I tell her how bad the thing is for her, she still insists on going on a sunbed every now and then) and Dad had a sauna. While I was steaming my way up and down the pool, I couldn't help wondering what Dan did at this time on a Saturday. Was he busy studying? Or perhaps he was cruising the chatroom looking for some other girl to chat up. Hmm.

On the way back home, Dad stopped off to get some videos to watch that night. Actually, he's got pretty good taste for someone so old. He got some really boring spy film but he did choose the latest Brad Pitt movie (he's so gorgeous!). So that had my evening sorted.

As soon as I got home, I dashed up to my room and logged on. The e-mail icon was flashing away. It was Butter, asking about French homework because she'd left her book at school on Friday. She'd sent the same e-mail to all of us and I was sure one of the gang would have got back to her already, but I replied anyway. Then I just couldn't resist a quick cruise around the chatroom. Well, I had to check it out to see if Dan was busy chatting to someone else, didn't I?

He wasn't. But he had been there. And left me a message!

```
Sam! Talk to me! Dan
```

It was at precisely that moment that Dad called up the stairs.

'Samantha? Phone. It's Claudia!'

Isn't it just typical of one of your best friends to call you at a really inconvenient moment? I went and got the cordless phone from him, and took it to my room.

'Claudia? How you doing?'

'I've just got back from the shops. I went with my cousin, you know, Carla? You'll never guess who we saw!'

'Robbie Williams?' I hadn't a clue but I knew that Claudia was going to tell me.

'Course not! We saw Mr Walker! In Gap!'

'Well, he's allowed to go shopping, isn't he? Even Maths teachers have to buy clothes, Claudia!'

'I know that, you moron. But he wasn't on his own! He was with a girl! She was really pretty. And he had his arm round her. They were almost snogging!' Claudia said it triumphantly.

'Get out of here! Mr Walker? A girl? Snogging? Yuck. What did she look like?'

'Blonde, long hair, slim, cool clothes. Much too good to be with Mr Walker.'

'No way! Any girl's too good to be with Mr Walker.' It's true, Mr Walker was . . . well, a teacher. Enough said. Claudia rabbited on in detail about what this poor girl was wearing, how tall she was, all that stuff.

'Then he saw us!'

'What, Walker did?'

'Yes! Carla and I were standing at the end of the shop and the two of them walked towards us. It was dead embarrassing when he suddenly realised I was there. He let go of her pretty quickly, I can tell you. Can't wait to see his face on Monday morning in Maths!'

We both giggled helplessly.

'Listen, got to go. I've only told you. Must tell Debs. See you. *Ciao*!'

Before I could even say goodbye, she was gone. I looked at my watch. I reckoned I had a couple of hours before Dad wanted to start watching the videos. Plenty of time to chat with Dan. Oh, and do some homework, of course.

Dan? You there?

The cursor kept winking at me but no one spoke. Was he out there?

Dan? It's Sam.

The cursor blinked and then there was a PLINK! noise. It was him!

Dan? How are you doing?

SAM, IS THAT YOU? D

Oh my God! It wasn't Dan it was Debs!

SAM? YOU THERE? D

Debs? Hi. How are u? S

WHO WERE YOU TALKING TO? WHO'S DAN? D

No one. S

That'd torn it. Now she knew I was talking to Dan.

WHO'S DAN IF HE'S NO ONE? D

Just someone I was talking to, that's all. S

YES?

The cursor blinked for a bit, then she said,

HOW LONG YOU BEEN TALKING TO HIM? D

What's the big deal? S

ISN'T ONE. BUT I THOUGHT WE JUST TALKED TO
EACH OTHER. D

**I just started chatting one day when I was
waiting for you lot. S**

Why wouldn't she just give it a rest? I could feel myself
blushing. Honestly, I really didn't need any of them knowing
about Dan. Not yet anyway. I mean, there wasn't much to tell
them anyway, was there?

YOU'D BETTER BE CAREFUL, SAM. THERE'S SOME
REAL WEIRDOS OUT THERE. D

OK, OK! Keep your hair on. You sound like Mum! S

I DO NOT! YOU'VE JUST GOT TO BE CAREFUL. D

She was referring to the chat we'd had in PHSE recently. Mrs Jones had been telling us all about the nutters that the police reckoned were out there surfing the net and trying to whisk us away.

I was only talking to him. OK? You spoken to Claudia? S

YES! IMAGINE SNOGGING WALKER! EUCH! D

There was a PLINK! I wondered if it was Dan. I really wanted it to be Dan. But I couldn't do anything about it, could I? Not with Debs and who knows who else around interfering. So I ignored the PLINK! and carried on talking to Debs for a bit. Then we both signed off, me using my homework as an excuse and Debs because she was going to see a film.

Charly leapt delicately on to my lap and purred. I was itching to see if Dan was there. But now I didn't dare, wondering who else amongst my friends was waiting to interrupt me. I slumped back in my chair. Oh, all right, then, so I was sulking!

I idled away the time for a few minutes, picking at my nails and twiddling my fingers around in my hair whilst I stared outside, watching my neighbours coming home from their

Saturdays in the dusk. For some reason I became engrossed in the man from three doors up, who was trying, unsuccessfully, to put what looked like a cupboard into the back of his car. It was obvious from where I was that the cupboard was way too big. But he kept turning it one way, then the other, trying to make it shrink.

PLINK! I jumped out of my reverie and looked at the screen, Charly delicately poking her claws into my trouser legs. She was telling me off, gently, for making her jump too. Words appeared on the screen in front of me.

Sam? You there? It's Dan. Sam?

Chapter 4

bbl
(Be back later)

Sam? You there?

Was I there? Of course I was but I wasn't sure if I could chat. You know, with my mates out there watching. They'd think I was some complete geek, wouldn't they? This sad girl who needed to chat to strangers on a Saturday night. The cursor blinked away at me.

Sam?

Oh, blow it, I wanted to talk to him. Find out more about him.

Dan?

Hi. Thought you weren't there. What you been up to?

Swimming, tennis. Not much. Listen, let's go private.

OK.

So off we went, into a 'room' on our own.

That's better. Sounds like more than not much to me. I play tennis too. Do you play at school?

Yes. But only in the summer. Otherwise I play at a club.

Sounds like you're good, then.

Wouldn't say that good, but I'm not that bad either. I'm going to try out for the school squad next term. How about you? You good?

OK. Pretty good at doubles. I play with a club too. It's good.

Where do you go to school?

It's a boys' school. A grammar. What's yours?

All girls' grammar.

So you're a girl-Sam, then!

I'd gone and told him without thinking! Well, he knew now.

Yeah. So what're you up to tonight?

Nothing much. Revising. More revising. And trying to avoid my little brother before I kill him!

It had to be him! I was convinced that Dan was 'Boy, 17'. But I had to know for sure.

So was it you who posted that 'Boy, 17' message I saw the other night?

You saw it! Yeah, I was going out of my mind . . .

So tell me about this brother you need rescuing from. How old is he?

13. He's OK sometimes but most of the time he's a pain, hence the rescue situation. How about you? Got any brothers?

No - no brothers or sisters. It's just me and my parents.

We chatted away for about half an hour. He asked all about

my mum and dad and it seemed OK to tell him. Then he told me all about his. He said his dad was a vet and that was what he wanted to do too when he left university. He was going to university to read Veterinary Science. I reckoned he had to be pretty bright. Most boys I know only have one ambition and that's to act like a moron. OK, OK, so I don't actually know that many boys. Butter's got brothers and they can be real geeks at times, though sometimes they're all right. Anyway, Dan sounded smart. And he sounded like he had a sense of humour too. He spoke about his brother and the things he got up to. He played loads of tricks on Dan and by the sound of it, Dan managed to catch him out sometimes too. In the end it was Dan who said he had to go.

My dad's got to go on a farm visit tonight. Said I'd go with him.

Farm visit? What for?

Some calves are due and he said he'd check on them for the farmer. So can I chat with you again, Sam?

Maybe. Another night, perhaps.

OK.

The cursor blinked and neither of us said anything. Oh God. Why had I been so cool again? So non-committal for the second time? I really wanted to talk to him. So why couldn't I just say so?

Perhaps we'll chat tomorrow? If I've got time in the evening?

Now was I looking too keen?

Perhaps. Gotta go. cu, Sam

cu. Bye

And he was gone.

But I thought about him all evening. Even though the videos Dad had got were really ace. Had I sounded desperate? Had I sounded too cool? What are you meant to do with some boy you meet in a chatroom? I don't know enough about them.

And I was still thinking about it when I got ready for bed that night. I wondered what the girls would do if they were in my shoes. I wondered if I could ask them. But then I decided that would be too embarrassing for words. Finally, I got under the duvet and finished this great novel I've been reading and switched off the light.

I lay there in the dark wondering what Dan looked like.

Was he blond? Thin or fat? Did he have long hair or a Number One? Oh my God! Perhaps he was short! Disaster! I'm five foot ten without shoes on. No, no, no, he couldn't be short.

Eventually I fell asleep.

I always think that Sundays are a mixture of really enjoyable laziness and total and utter boredom. I'd really like to be able to hang out with someone else but like I said, all my girlfriends live quite a way away so, unless you plan in advance it's a bit difficult to get to see them all. We do that in the holidays but during term time we don't so much, mostly because of homework and stuff.

Anyway, on this Sunday I did what I do on most Sundays. Pretended to tidy my room, got my bag ready for school the next day, practised the piano with my dad whistling in accompaniment in the other room (so irritating but I don't really complain that much), more homework and some GCSE project stuff, curled up on the sofa with Charly while I started a new book, watched the telly and then tiptoed out of the living-room past Mum and Dad who had both fallen asleep on the sofa with the Sunday papers piled on top of them.

I went back up to my room and switched on my PC. Surprise, surprise – I had mail. It must be the girls.

I was right. I went into my in-box and sure enough there were five messages . . .

From: butter@friedeggs.com
To: sam@newshoes.com

Sam! Who is this boy you've been chatting to? Isn't Mr Walker disgusting? Phone me!

From: claudia@raginglooney.co.uk
To: sam@newshoes.com

Debs has told me all about this boy Dan. Is this wise, Sam? Is he gorgeous? Can you imagine Walker snogging? Aaaaaaah!

From: debs@doobopdaloola.com
To: sam@newshoes.com

I've been thinking about this boy, Sam. You'd better not give too much away about yourself. And how come you got to him before the rest of us did?

Typical! They all had to interfere. I sulked around my room for a bit, determined that I wasn't going to reply to them. They could all stew until Monday because sure as eggs are eggs they were going to get at me first thing at school. Friends – one minute you want to hug them and the next you want to strangle them!

At least I knew that none of them would be able to ring me about it on Sunday with the rest of our families around listening in. And I kept my mobile switched off so that they couldn't get messages to me until the next day. Huh! That had got them sorted.

I went and played the piano some more to let off steam: a really loud crashing piece of Rachmaninov that I could only play part of. But the bit that I could play was dead dramatic so that got it out of my system – until Mum came in, woken from her sofa slumber by the noise and asking if I really had to keep my foot so hard down on the loud pedal. She probably had a point. But by then I was feeling a bit better and I helped her make some supper for us and chilled out a bit.

Later, in the bath, I wondered if Dan's friends would interfere so much about him talking to me. But then perhaps he didn't have any friends. Perhaps he really was some geek who had to get his kicks out of the internet.

No! Dan wasn't like that. I was sure he wasn't. But I wasn't sure how to find out for definite.

After my bath I realised that I hadn't switched off my PC and the screen saver was still whizzing round. I was just about to shut it down and get into bed but I couldn't resist the urge to go into the chatroom. After all, if Dan was a geek, he might be busy chatting away right this very minute to some other girl, mightn't he?

He wasn't. He wasn't even there. But he had been. Earlier that day. And he'd left me a message:

```
Sam: Can't chat this evening but would
like to speak again. Monday night, if
that's OK with you. Dan.
```

Oh no! What if one of the girls had seen it too!

Chapter 5

ruok?
(Are you OK?)

'So come on, then, spill the beans.' Debs put her arm through mine as I walked through the school gate.

'Yes, come on, tell us. Who is he?' Butter and Claudia followed alongside us. It was Monday morning and I got the feeling that they'd all been waiting, ready to pounce, for some time.

'Who's who? Spill what beans?' As if I didn't know what they were talking about!

'This boy, Dan . . .?' Claudia asked penetratingly.

'Yes Dan, who is he?' Now Debs was joining in as well.

Was there nothing else in the world of interest on a Monday morning? Was no one interested in whether the Blues would win the Cup or if Madonna's new video was the bizz? I wasn't at all sure what to say. Actually, I felt a bit embarrassed. After all, I hardly knew Dan, did I? And I wasn't sure I wanted to talk about him anyway on the main walk into school in front of the whole world.

'He's just some boy, OK! I got talking to him the other night when I was waiting for you lot to turn up in the chat-room. You didn't and he did. So we got talking. Satisfied?'

'So how old is he, then?' Butter asked. 'And where does he come from?' She sounded just like some old lady at the supermarket checkout.

'He's seventeen and he lives in the Midlands somewhere. He's wants to be a vet and he's got a brother who's thirteen. Other than that there's not much else to tell. We've chatted a couple of times and he seems really nice. If you want to know any more, I can't give it to you. Mostly because I haven't had a chance to find out any more.'

Well, it was sort of true, wasn't it? I could feel myself blushing.

'He could be any old perv!' spluttered Claudia. 'There was a story in the paper the other day about some girl in America who got raped by some guy she met on the internet!'

Oh, great. This was really making me feel good. Not only did they all know about Dan but now they were trying to make him out to be some weirdo. 'Look, I'm still here, aren't I? He hasn't managed to do anything to me, has he? Anyway, what makes you so sure he must be so bad? I mean, we chat on the internet, don't we? Are we loonies?'

'Yes, she's right,' said Debs. 'Give her a break, Claudia. All she's done is chat to some boy from the safety of her PC.'

'Well . . .' Claudia stumbled.

'But it's different,' said Butter.

'It is? Why?' I wasn't going to let them get away that easily. Even if they were my friends.

'Well . . . We only talk to each other, don't we?' Butter was very satisfied with her answer. So was Claudia, who nodded sagely in agreement.

'And can you honestly say that neither of you have ever chatted to someone you don't know in a chatroom?' demanded Debs. 'I certainly have.'

'Exactly!'

Apart from a couple of splutters there was silence from the other two. They couldn't look us in the eye.

'Hah! I was right! You hypocrites!' I accused.

'I've only spoken to boys when they've been part of a group chat,' said Claudia.

'So what's the big difference?' I said indignantly.

'Well, why didn't you tell us about him?' said Claudia.

'Yes, you kept him a secret!' Butter joined in.

'Hardly a secret with you lot around! I'd only just spoken to him when you all found out about him!' It was so ridiculous that even I started to laugh at the thought of keeping anything a secret from that lot. The others laughed as well. By which time we'd arrived at our classroom. Only just in time for registration.

'Tell us more about him later!' hissed Butter as we sat down at our desks ready for Mrs Jason, our form tutor, to start registration.

What more was there to tell them? I thought as I sat there, half-listening for my name. They practically knew as much about him as I did. But I kept thinking about everything they'd said about all those weirdos in the papers. What if Dan was an old perv? How was I going to find out? Truly, every time I let myself think about it during the school day, I shivered at the thought.

By lunch-time, the girls *definitely* knew as much about Dan as I did! After a typical Monday, I walked to the bus stop with Debs, who was on the way to meet her mum somewhere.

We talked about the gospel choir that Debs was dead keen to get into. It's really well-known – they've made CDs and even been on a tour of Europe. Debs has set her heart on getting into it, but she's got to wait two more years before she'll be old enough to audition. Meantime, Debs had got hold of a video of the choir and she was going to watch it that weekend and dream. Then we got into Friday's episode of 'Friends'. It's probably our number one programme, although it does compete with 'The Simpsons'.

Then Debs said, 'So, are you going to chat with Dan again tonight?'

'Oh, I don't know. The way you lot laid into me today I expect you'll all be there, eyes agog, looking in, won't you?'

'We did go on a bit, Sam. Sorry. Listen, we're only worried about you getting hurt.' She gave me a hug as we both threw our bags down at the queue at the bus stop.

'Still, if you ask me, we're all a bit jealous that you found Dan before we did. I'm sure all of us would have chatted to him if we'd got to him first!'

'Would you?'

'Certain of it. I mean, if you found his message attractive why wouldn't we? Stands to reason.'

I grinned at the thought of having Dan to myself. 'You really think so?'

'Sure do. Anyway, I think it sounds dead romantic. I mean, he's probably really good-looking and cool! And,' she rolled her eyes dramatically, 'he's seventeen! How many of us lot have even spoken to a boy who's seventeen? Except when he's our brother?'

I could see my bus approaching and picked up my bag. I grinned at Debs. 'Well, maybe you're right. See you tomorrow.'

I boarded the bus and miraculously seemed to win one of the fights for a seat.

All the way home I wondered whether Dan really could be good-looking and romantic.

When I got home, Charly came sidling up the garden path to greet me. She was nearly always waiting for me like that when I came home from school. It didn't matter what time I got home, Charly had this kind of sixth sense that told her exactly when to wake from her slumber in the bushes in time to have a good stretch before I opened the gate.

Inside the house, she went off to find her water bowl and I flicked on the kettle to make a cup of tea and then search the fridge for some sustenance. OK, so I'm lucky that I don't have to be too careful about what I eat. I know that. But remember, I am also five foot ten so the calories have a long way to travel!

Appetite suppressed, I went up to my room. My room, by the way, is totally cool: I painted it a kind of aubergine colour with Mum and I've got this really great duvet cover and stuff that Mum found in some shop in the West End. The girls think it looks really cool too.

It's probably a bit tragic, but I like to keep my school uniform on when I do my homework – somehow it makes me feel more in a work mode. But once the really tedious stuff is done, I change into my jeans and relax a bit.

That day was no exception and I took all my books out of

my school bag. I decided to tackle History in uniform and do my English essay in jeans. I looked at my watch and wondered what time Dan would be in the chatroom. Perhaps he'd be there now? I logged on and tapped in the address.

The bright logo of the chatroom zoomed into view but I couldn't see a message from Dan anywhere. For a second I thought about leaving a message myself but then I changed my mind. The girls were likely to arrive any minute and I'd had more than enough of them for one day, thanks. I didn't even feel like chatting to any of them.

Almost telepathically there was a PLINK! and Claudia was there. She was quickly followed by Butter and Debs. Then they went off into one of the private 'rooms' to chat. I sat watching the main arrivals room for a bit longer but Dan never showed. In the end I got on with my History but I had butterflies in my stomach the whole time.

'Samantha? Hi! I'm home!' It was Mum and she had pretty good timing because I'd just finished my History and was changing into my jeans.

I thundered down the stairs. 'Hi, how was your day?'

'Not so bad actually. I took on a new case today. A sweet little toddler whose mum died last year. She's never seen her dad and now her grandmother, who's looking after her, wants to adopt her.'

'How old's the little girl?' I asked.

'She's only two. And so pretty and adorable.' Mum put her briefcase down and hung her coat on the hook. 'Actually, she reminded me of you when you were that age.'

'Aww – don't tell me she was chubby-cheeked and had dark hair with a bow on the top!' I mimicked the excrutiatingly cute hairstyle that my mum had put me into for a studio photograph she'd had done of me. Embarrassing or what!

'Yes, darling!' Mum giggled because she knew I couldn't bear it if anyone spotted the photograph in the living-room. 'So, how about you? Good day? Lots of homework?'

'Yes, on both counts! But I've done History and I'm just about to start on English. Is it OK with you if I get on with it while you do supper?'

'Course. We'll eat in about an hour, OK?'

'A whole hour! I don't think I can last that long.' I grabbed a banana from the fruit bowl in the kitchen. 'See you later!'

I really like English so it wasn't a problem for me to get into the essay. It was done in forty minutes and I shut my folder in satisfaction and stretched myself just like Charly. I still had my piano practice to do, but that was fun so it didn't really count. Unable to resist, I went back into the chatroom. Would Dan be taking a break from his studying, I wondered.

There was a selection of messages posted in the arrivals room, but there wasn't one from Dan. I was surprised at how disappointed I felt. I wondered if any of the girls were there, because I knew that despite what I'd thought about them earlier, I could always rely on them to comfort me. I looked round and couldn't see any evidence of them. I glanced at my watch. Well, it was only seven o'clock. Perhaps I was too early for Dan. That thought made me feel a bit better. It also made me feel determined.

Hi, Dan? You out there?

The cursor gave its cheeky little blink at me. Then someone came in!

HELLO? WHO'S THAT?

Huh! Who's that? Did he chat to lots of people, then?

It's Sam. Hi, how are you?

IT'S NOT DAN, SAM. I'M STEVE. GOOD TO TALK TO YOU. YOU DON'T MIND CHATTING TO ME, DO YOU?

The cheek! Who was this Steve? I certainly didn't want to talk to him!

Sorry. Looking for someone else. Bye

**DON'T GO, SAM! I'D LIKE TO CHAT. YOU A BOY OR
A GIRL? HOW OLD ARE YOU?**

Oh boy, not again! I wasn't having it. I didn't want Steve! I
wanted Dan!

Sorry. Gotta go! BYE!

**SAM? SAM? PLEASE DON'T GO! SAM? DO YOU PREFER
BIKINIS OR SWIMSUITS?**

What? This was creepy. Bikinis? What was this guy on? How
did he even know I was a girl?

I looked at the cursor key blinking defiantly at me. I wasn't
going to reply. Perhaps he'd get the hint. But he didn't. He
kept pestering and asking me to chat. Then suddenly he was
wiped from the screen. Presumably by whoever was
monitoring the chatroom. Thank goodness! I felt cold but I
was relieved to have got out of that one. I was about to go
off-line, feeling miserable about not speaking to Dan, when
a new message appeared:

`Hi, Sam! You there?`

Oh no, he was back!

`Sam? It's Dan. You there?`

Was it really Dan or was it the pesky Steve again?

Sam! If you're there say hi. I need
rescuing from my brother!

Steve couldn't know about Dan's brother. I tell you, I
positively leaped to that keyboard!

Dan, hi! It's Sam.

I thought for a minute you weren't there!

**I tried to talk b4 but some bloke butted in.
You weren't around.**

Sorry. Am now - let's go private!

Once we were in the room, Dan and I caught up with each
other's news. I told him about my friends thinking that he
might be a nutter.

Glad they've got such faith in me! So tell
me more about your tennis. Do you reckon
you're going to make it into the school
squad, then?

**I might do, but I'll have to get some more
practise in. There's a tennis camp in the next
holiday. I'm not sure if I want to go or not
though.**

Tennis camp? You're kidding. Where is it?
I'm going on one next holiday. Do you
think it's the same one?

It couldn't be, could it? I mean, when did you last have such good luck? I never have!

**It's at that new sports college in
Leicestershire. You know, the one where they
did all the training before the Olympics last
year?**

I don't believe it. It's the one I'm going
to. Hope you do come. Then perhaps we'll
meet.

I haven't booked it yet.

Yet? I hadn't even agreed with Mum that I was going to go. But now that I knew Dan was going, I was certain that I wanted to!

Please say yes! Then we can talk properly.

I'll let you know about it.

I thought I really sounded cool!

> Listen, would you mind if I took your e-
> mail address? Then we could chat without
> berks like Steve and your mates butting
> in.

Hmm. Now this was making things more personal. But I really felt I'd got to know Dan a bit and that I could trust him. I didn't reckon I could come to any harm if I gave him my e-mail address. So I did. And he gave me his too. Then we were interrupted by my mum calling me to eat.

Gotta go, Dan. Grub's up.

> Sure. Listen, good to talk to you and
> please say you'll come to tennis camp! And
> swap e-mails.

OK, I'll think about it. Bye

> Bye!

Mum and I chatted over supper as usual although I did find it difficult because I was too excited for words to think that Dan and I might end up at the same tennis camp together! What kind of coincidence was that! Out of this world, I bet. In the end, I couldn't bear thinking about it any longer.

  'Mum? You know that tennis camp we were talking about?

Well, I wondered if I could go.'

'What's brought on this sudden change of mind, then?'

'I just thought it might be a way of building on what I'll learn if I get into the school tennis squad this summer, that's all.' OK, so I fibbed a bit but it was sort of true.

'Sounds like a good idea to me, darling. I'm sure that Dad will agree too. Of course you can go, Samantha. I'll ring up the club tomorrow from work and book a place for you.'

'Thanks, Mum!' I couldn't stop myself grinning from ear to ear.

'Are any of your friends going as well, Samantha?'

'No, why should they?'

'No particular reason. Except that you weren't so keen to go because you said you wouldn't know anyone there.'

Good grief! Could my mother have possibly earwigged in on my conversation with Dan? Of course she couldn't have, I realised. But it was spooky – and embarrassing, too!

'Of course I don't know anyone else that's going. How could I?' I could feel myself blushing right down into my boots.

Now I couldn't wait for supper to be over and to get back upstairs to my room. I had fibbed to my mum. But it was only a little incey-wincey fib, wasn't it? I mean, I didn't actually know Dan yet, did I?

* * *

In the bath that night an idea suddenly struck me. I had Dan's e-mail address, didn't I? I could e-mail him with the news about the camp! I leaped out of the bath, dried myself, dressed and was in the bedroom, on-line, within minutes.

From: sam@newshoes.com
To: danjbrown@sooper.net
Dan,
Mum says I can go on the tennis camp!
cu there. Sam

It was only when I got into bed and settled down to read my novel that I had second thoughts about my impulsive e-mail. Had I been too keen? Oh no!

Chapter 6

bcnu
(Be seeing you)

The next day, the morning at school passed in a daze. I found myself constantly thinking about Dan: supposing he thought I was a complete geek for sending that e-mail to him? Supposing he thought I was desperate? Supposing he was one of those boys that you hear about who get turned off by girls who do some of the running? The girls kept on at me all day, asking me what I was dreaming about. Somehow, I managed to dodge the issue because of lessons. But at lunch-time, Debs and I had to go to the school library to fetch some books we'd ordered for Music (we were both doing Music GCSE as an extra subject: just like I do piano, Debs does the clarinet).

'So what's up, Sam?'

'What?' I pretended I didn't know what she was talking about.

'What's up? You've been going around like a wet weekend all day. Something's wrong. Come on, tell Aunty Debs?'

'Nothing . . . really. Nothing . . .'

'Don't believe you, Sam.' She put her arms round me. 'Nothing to do with lover-boy, is it? You know, Mr Love Chat?' She laughed and then it was obvious that she realised she'd got straight to the point. 'Seriously, Sam, is it? He hasn't dumped you already, has he?'

As if! 'No he has not!'

'So why the glum face all day, then? You're hardly your usual cheerful self, are you? Go on, you know I won't blab to the others. Just as long, that is, as when I tell you my secret, you won't tell either.'

'What secret?' What was she on about?

'Like I said, you tell me yours and I'll tell you mine. You go first,' Debs smiled and tilted her head to one side expectantly.

So I told her all about my chat with Dan and how I'd decided to go on the tennis camp. And, of course, my big mistake about sending the e-mail.

'So, what's the big deal? Has he e-mailed back with some stupid remark or something?'

'No, I haven't heard from him since.'

'So when did you send the e-mail, then?'

'Last night.'

'What, and you're already worried about him not getting back to you? Give the bloke a chance! Presumably he had to go to school this morning like you, didn't he? So when's he meant to have replied?'

But before I could answer, Miss Manx, the librarian, came over to us and hissed, 'Ahem! This is supposed to be a library, girls. A place of private and quiet study! If you two want to gossip, I suggest that you do that in another place. It's lunch-time, after all. If you want to talk, go and do it in your form room.'

'Sorry, miss.' I scrabbled my books together and went over to the desk to sign them out. I could hear Debs apologising behind me and scuttling out too.

Once we were outside, Debs started again, as we walked slowly towards the next lesson after lunch.

'So what's all this rubbish about waiting for Mr E-mail to come to you, Sam?'

'It's not like that,' I protested. 'It's just that I've made an idiot of myself, haven't I, by looking so keen.'

'You what? Sam – you can do what you like!'

I tried again to explain. But as I did, I began to see Debs's point. I mean, why shouldn't I e-mail Dan?

'OK, Debs, you're right. I mean, if Dan doesn't like me e-mailing him, that's tough.' I had to admit that I felt better for talking to someone about it. Then I remembered that Debs had something to tell me. 'So, go on, then – tell me the Big Secret.'

'Well,' she said dramatically as she linked her arm through mine, 'remember I told you about that choir that was coming to visit our church this Sunday? Well, I went to see them with my gran. And there was this gorgeous boy there!'

'You're kidding! What's he like? Did you speak to him?'

'Pretty good-looking actually. And with really cool clothes. He sang a solo. And I got the chance to speak to him after the service when we all had this kind of supper thing in the hall.'

'And are you going to see him again?'

'Actually yes, in a couple of weeks' time when our choir goes to visit his church. It's near that boys' school where they wear black blazers. That's the school he goes to. So do two of his brothers.'

'So you found out quite a bit about him, then.'

'Certainly did. And we exchanged e-mail addresses so I hope to find out even more.' She grinned a very pleased-with-herself smile. 'But don't tell the others, OK?'

'Fair do's. As long as you keep quiet too.'

'Promise – I told you. Now come on, or we'll be late for French.'

It was during French though that I suddenly thought: at least Debs knew that her boy was good-looking. Supposing Dan was ugly? Or maybe he wasn't going to e-mail me back and then he'd be at the tennis camp and he'd ignore me. Now *that* would be really boring.

When I got home, I got my usual greeting from Charly and, armed with a cup of tea and some toast, I headed for my room and switched on my PC.

My mail in-box had something in it! After giving Charly an extra-special hug, I placed her carefully at the end of my bed and went back to the PC. There were butterflies in my stomach as I opened up my mail. But apparently I had a message from someone called stevecooper@groovyserve. Oh no, not that nutter who'd tried to chat with me the other night? Perhaps the girls were right and somehow, by going into the chatroom the way I had, I had invited some weirdos into the world of my PC.

I opened up the mail, wondering if some internet virus was going to take me over. And there it was:

From: stevecooper@groovyserve.com
To: sam@newshoes.com
Sam, it's Dan. My PC's gone down and I'm using my friend Steve's laptop to e-mail you. Wondered if we could talk tonight? Can you ring me on my mobile, 0321 32112. Dan

Talk to him? Tonight? For real rather than via the internet?

Well, I wasn't at all sure. I mean, what was I going to say to him? What was he going to say to me? Now what the hell was I going to do?

I worried about it all through supper. Mum even asked me whether I was feeling OK. I told her that I had a headache which was a little bit true, and used it as an excuse to go back up to my room. Mum, as usual, had some work to do, so I knew that she would be heavily involved, working on her laptop for most of the evening.

Once I was in my bedroom, I got so jittery at the thought of phoning Dan that I did actually feel ill. First of all, I even began to tidy my room. I'd do anything to avoid making a decision about whether or not I was going to call Dan! But after I'd excavated the murky depths beneath my bed I couldn't make any more excuses. I'd run out of avoidance tactics. Except for going to the loo and making sure, by leaning over the stairs and trying to peer through the living-room doorway, that Mum was still at work. She was.

I switched on my mobile. I had two text messages. One was from Debs:

> **have u hurd?**
> **I hav!**

The other was from Claudia:

```
uok? seemd sad
     2day.
```

That was typical of them! I sent a message back to Claudia
straight away:

```
fine thx.
headache.
cu 2morrow.
```

But I didn't send a message back to Debs. I thought I'd wait
until I did or didn't decide I had the courage to phone Dan.

So next I checked my PC. I had more mail in my in-box.

From: butter@friedeggs.com
To: sam@newshoes.com

Why aren't you chatting?!

There was no way I was going to reply. But I went back into
Dan's e-mail. There was his mobile number. I looked at the
time on my bedside clock. It was just after eight o'clock. Heck,
he probably wasn't going to be around anyway. I picked up
my mobile and dialled Dan's number.

It rang once.

'Hello?'

I was expecting a message service and this seemed like

a real voice. I couldn't think of an answer.

'Hello?' There was the voice again. Was it Dan? Had I got the right number? Whoever it was, they didn't sound too bad. 'Hello? Is that you, Sam?'

Oh boy, he said my name! It *was* Dan. 'Hello, Sam?'

'Yes, it's Sam.' What an idiot! Just when I wanted to sound so cool and sophisticated!

'Hi, Sam. Glad you could call me. How are you doing?' He sounded so sweet. I mean, not like a weirdo, just cute. In a nice way.

'Hi. Fine, thanks. How about you?'

'Sorry about my computer. It's been a real bummer having to borrow my mate's laptop. Hope you didn't mind me sending you the e-mail but I really wanted to talk to you. I didn't want you to think that I was ignoring you.' Dan sounded apologetic.

'No problem. So how long's your machine been down, then?' I was pleased that I sounded so together.

'Oh, just since last night. There's a problem with the phones here. My dad's going bonkers – it affects his business, you see, being a vet.'

Dan sounded so nice. After all the worry about chatting to him, he was actually really easy to talk to once I'd taken the plunge. We chatted away mobile to mobile about all sorts of things: school, his dad's work as a vet, his mum, who

74

was a district nurse. Then he asked me about my mum and dad so I told him. It wasn't any effort at all. It was just like I'd known him for a long time.

'So did you get my e-mail, then?' Dan hadn't mentioned it so far.

'No! When did you send it? I haven't got my messages for a day or two. Did you e-mail? What was it about?'

Blast! He hadn't got it. And here was me worrying all day about it, what he thought of it!

'Sam, you still there?'

'Yes.'

'So what did you e-mail me about?'

'Oh, just the tennis camp we were talking about. I've booked.'

'Sam, that's great! It'll be really good to see you there.' I couldn't believe how genuinely pleased he sounded. After all that worry it seemed like it was OK. Debs was right! 'Will you be there for the two weeks?'

'Yes, I think so. It'll be good to get the chance to meet you.'

'And you. But listen, that's a couple of months away – we should meet up before then, don't you think?'

'What?' Was I really hearing this? 'How? I mean, it's not as if you live close by, is it?'

'I know. That's what I've been thinking about. It would be

great to meet up somewhere soon. I've thought a lot about it and I reckon we could meet up at that new shopping centre that's just been opened – you know, the Waterside that's at the junction of all the motorways? I thought we could meet up there as a kind of halfway point between us. What do you say?'

Can you believe he was saying this? He'd obviously worked it all out and it all sounded so simple. And he sounded so nice that I ended up saying, 'Yes – sounds like a good idea. But when? I mean, I can't do it next weekend because we've got to go to some do at my gran's.'

'Well, let's try for the weekend after that. I don't think I've got anything on then. I worked it out on the map. You can get the train from near you and go straight to the shopping centre. It'd be really good to meet you at last.'

'Yes, it would.' Then I realised how that sounded. 'I mean, it would be good to meet you too.'

There was silence. Had I said the wrong thing again? 'Dan? You still there?'

'Listen, I've got to go. My mum's calling me downstairs. Speak to you soon, Sam. And don't forget to put that date in your diary.'

'Yes, bye!'

And the phone went dead. Did he say date? Did Dan and I have a date?

I went and snuggled up with Charly on my bed. Had this conversation really happened? Apparently it had. And then suddenly it dawned on me. It was all very well me making the arrangements with Dan but how was I going to get this one past my mum? Oh, no ...

Chapter 7

: -}
(Embarrassed)

Later on, Mum came in to check how I was.

'You feeling better, Samantha?'

'Yes, thanks. I've finished all my work so I think I'll have an early night. Night, Mum.'

'Night, Samantha. Sleep well.' She kissed me goodnight and wandered along the hall to the bathroom.

Well, it was true that I'd done my work. It's just that I hadn't really done it very well because I'd spent most of my time wondering how I was going to actually get to meet Dan. I mean, I could lie and tell Mum that I was going to the centre with the girls, but that would be rather dodgy. Then I wondered about saying I had to go to a concert with Mrs Jay. But that would be equally dodgy. In the end, I gave myself a real headache worrying about it and fell asleep with exhaustion.

The next morning after breakfast, just as I was leaving the house, I got a text message:

```
Good 2 talk 2
  u last nite.
  cu in 2 wks.
When and where?
 spk 2u 2nite.
     Dan
```

I felt myself tingle all over. Dan J Brown, 17, seemed awfully keen on me. And it felt good.

I can't remember the journey to school at all. I think I sat on the bus in a daze. I don't even remember showing my pass to the conductor. But I did get there and found the girls already in the classroom, listening to Debs telling them all about the boy that she'd met at church and had been e-mailing. So much for that being a secret! I panicked – supposing she'd told them all about me and Dan?

The bell rang for assembly and we all trooped off to the hall. I linked my arm through Debs's as we made our way through the throng of gibbering girls.

'I thought it was a big secret, Debs!'

'Well, it *was* but only for a short while. But don't worry, I haven't said a thing about your e-boy. Anyway, have you heard from him?'

I told her all about it.

'Fantastic! But how are you going to get there?'

I only just about had time to tell her my worries about telling Mum when we arrived at assembly. And you know what teachers are like about talking in assembly. As we sat down, Debs whispered, 'Tricky one,' into my ear. Then the school day began and I immersed myself in it so I could ignore the problem for the rest of the day. Except at lunchtime, when the girls all asked me if I'd heard from Dan. I told them all about the phone call and how great he sounded. I wanted them to know he wasn't a geek.

'You lucky old thing, Sam,' Butter said. 'I bet if I'd met some boy like that he'd probably turn out to have nothing to say for himself in real life.'

'And me,' said Claudia. 'OK, I'll come clean. I went into the chatroom last night and there were boys and I was chatting to them but they were totally pants. You know, lads that think it's really cool to type in obscene words and behave like morons all the time.'

'I know,' said Butter, 'I've watched dorks like that before. There's no point in trying to chat to them. They're just awful!'

'They really were the pits,' sighed Claudia. 'Unlike Sam's boy, it seems.'

Butter giggled along with Claudia. 'Well, better to find the morons in a chatroom than at the school's Christmas disco!' Then we all giggled again, remembering some boys we'd met at the last one and who'd tried to get us to dance with them. They were so disgusting and so arrogant!

It was really good to be part of this bunch of friends. Even when you were feeling really bad about something, someone would always say something and make you feel better. I wondered if I should tell them about meeting Dan and see what advice they might have. I was lucky that he hadn't turned out to be bad news on the phone. But what was I going to do about meeting him? He was going to ring me again tonight and I was no closer to having sorted it.

When I got home from school that afternoon I went straight to the piano (after saying hello to Charly, of course). I often find that bashing out a dramatic piece of music takes the steam out of me. It sort of worked – and it kept me away from the phone in case Dan rang before I could think of what to say to him about our date. I still couldn't believe that Dan had called it a date. That was what girlfriends and boyfriends had, and he and I hadn't even seen each other yet.

Anyway, I was still working at the piano when Mum came in.

'Hello, love.' She popped her head around the door. 'OK?'

'Fine thanks, Mum. You?'

'Oh – a very long day in court. And it's day two tomorrow, which I'm not looking forward to at all. Anyway,

I'm just going to go up and change and then I'll get supper.'

'OK, I'll just finish this piece.'

I carried on with my music with half an ear out on what Mum was up to. As soon as I heard her coming back down and going into the kitchen, I closed the lid on the piano and went and joined her.

'Thought you might like some help, Mum. What can I do?'

'Oh, that would be nice. Can you prepare some vegetables for me, sweetheart?'

I got the stuff out of the fridge and got to work. I can't pretend I'm really into cooking, but I suppose at least I know what to do with some veg and a knife and chopping board.

I'd been brewing up what to say to Mum all the time I'd been on the piano. Suddenly, I couldn't stop myself and I went for it, probably too hastily.

'Mum? You know that tennis camp?'

'Oh yes, love, I meant to say – I called the club during my lunch break today and I've reserved you a place. It's all booked.'

'Oh, thanks, Mum. Actually it wasn't really about going that I wanted to talk to you. It's just that I've met this boy who's also going to the camp and we'd like to meet up at that new Waterside shopping centre – you know, the one that we were reading about in the Sunday papers – in a couple of weeks' time. That's OK, isn't it?'

'Sorry, Samantha,' Mum put a saucepan of water on the stove to boil, 'which boy is this? Is he someone at the tennis club? Why do you have to go all the way to that place to meet him? It's miles away.'

'Oh he doesn't live around here. He lives up in the Midlands. The shopping centre is a mid-way place for both of us. That's why we thought it would be a good place to meet.' I could see from Mum's face that she was puzzled, and I rushed on. 'So that's OK, is it? Thanks, Mum.' There, I'd sorted it!

But that's not what Mum thought.

'Sorry, Samantha, but exactly how have you met this boy if he lives in the Midlands? I don't understand.'

'Well, he's someone I've known for a couple of weeks, actually. And then I found out quite by accident that he's going to the tennis camp too. Isn't it an amazing coincidence!' I didn't even look up at Mum in case she looked me in the eye. I just carried on with my peeling and chopping.

'But, Samantha, where did you actually meet him? You haven't been on any school trips lately, have you? Certainly not in the last couple of weeks.'

When you've got a mother who is smart, there's not a lot that slips by her without being noticed.

'So, come on, Samantha, where did you meet him?'

'Oh, it was just an amazing coincidence. We met when I was talking with the girls on the internet.' I slopped the vegetables into the saucepan Mum had given me and started to fill the pan with water. The noise of the rushing water from the tap unfortunately didn't drown out Mum's interrogation. Honestly, she'd have made a good barrister.

'You met this boy via the internet? Samantha, now I know that you and your friends have chats on there but you know that your dad and I have expressly forbidden you to talk to other people in those chatrooms. You know that. We've had long talks about it. We've read all about those perverts who prey on people via the internet in the paper. Samantha, you really disappoint me.'

Ouch! That hurt!

'Mum, he's a nice boy! He's not some weirdo. He's seventeen and he's studying to go to university to be a vet, like his dad. He's got a younger brother and his mum is a community nurse. He sounds really nice – perfectly normal, not a monster. So when he asked me if I could meet him it sounded like a really good idea.'

'You've spoken to this boy? Samantha, you must be mad! Anything could have happened to you!'

'What, over a mobile phone? How?'

'Well, you know what I mean, Samantha! You have to be really careful with these people. We've all read about people posing as someone perfectly innocent and then turning out to be truly dangerous. I'm glad he seemed nice on the phone but I'm not at all happy about you giving out your mobile phone number over the internet.'

'I didn't! He e-mailed me his! That's how we got in touch!' I was getting really indignant now. Did she think I was a complete idiot?

'You gave your e-mail address to a complete stranger? Oh, Samantha!' Mum was beginning to raise her voice and she didn't do that very often. She was very controlled usually. This was a bad sign.

'Oh well, if that's how you feel about it!' I slammed down my knife and a carrot and stomped off to my room.

I blew that one, didn't I?

I was slumped on my bed when Mum came in a few minutes later.

'Samantha? Can I come in?'

'Looks like you already are!' I regretted it as soon as I said it.

'Come on, Samantha. I think we can both do better than we already have, don't you? I'm sorry I got cross downstairs.' Mum sat down at the foot of the bed and stroked Charly, whose purrs got louder and louder. 'So you've spoken to this boy on the phone and he sounds nice. So when does he want to meet you?'

'In two weekends' time. Can I go, then?'

'Well, I'd like to know more about this boy before I say yes. I think perhaps I should speak to his parents, don't you?'

'Mum!' I sat bolt upright on the bed. 'You cannot be serious! You cannot humiliate me in this way! I'm fifteen, for goodness sake!'

'Exactly, Samantha! You are fifteen and he is seventeen – or so he says. If he's the decent boy you say he is,' I was spluttering with rage,' – and I am sure that he is – then he won't mind if I speak to his mother, will he? After all, he'd want you to be safe, wouldn't he?'

I was like, 'hello?' I couldn't speak. I was so angry! I was so embarrassed! I wanted to leave home immediately!

'Samantha? Do you have his number? I'll phone him tonight for you.'

'Oh no you won't! Can you imagine it! You calling my friend? No thanks.'

'Well, I'm sorry but I won't agree to the meeting until I speak to his mother or father. I'm sure your dad would agree with me too. It's up to you, Samantha.' Mum was looking at me.

'No way!'

'OK, have it your own way, Samantha. I'm going downstairs to cook supper. I'll call you when it's ready.'

I lay back on my bed as she shut the door. She was back in control again, not shouting or slamming the door. Unlike me. Charly came up and snuggled her head against my cheek. At least Charly never got cross with me. She never seemed disappointed with me.

I lay there thinking for a few minutes and the phone rang. It was so quiet in my room that the musical ring made me jump with surprise. I leaned over and picked the phone out of my school bag. The number on the screen was Dan's!

Without stopping to think, I answered the call to stop the phone's incessant ringing tune.

'Hello, Dan?'

'Hi! How are you doing?'

'Fine – well, actually, not fine.'

'Why, what's happened to you?'

I told him all about the row with Mum.

'Bummer! Hey look, you can kind of see her point though, can't you?'

'Yes, I suppose, but she's wrong though, isn't she?'

'What, you mean I haven't told you that I'm three feet tall, ten stone, have got black teeth and have a propensity to eat small children?'

I laughed. Dan really did seem like a decent bloke.

'But she wants to talk to your mum! To check up on you!'

'Well . . . I don't think my mum will spill the beans about all of my bad habits. I think she quite likes me because I'm her son and all that.'

'But will she want to speak to my mum?'

We talked about the problem for a while and then Dan said, 'Looks like we haven't got a choice though, doesn't it? I mean, if we don't let our mums talk, then we can't meet until the tennis camp. And, of course, because you've told your mum about us meeting at the camp, there's a possibility of your mum not wanting us to meet there either if she still thinks I'm a weirdo.'

I hadn't thought of that! 'Suppose not. So what are we going to do?'

'Got a pen and some paper?'

I grabbed some from my desk. 'Yes.' And I took down Dan's home phone number.

'I'll tell my mum to expect your mum's call. But it might be an idea if she waits until tomorrow to call her. That way I can prepare my mum for the news.'

'OK. Thanks, Dan.'

'No problem. It was good to talk to you, Sam. Now, I'd better go and get in a spot of howling outside the window before supper. Us werewolves need to keep in practice, you know!'

I laughed and could hear Dan pretending to howl as I said goodbye and hung up. Sorted! Now all I had to do was hope that Dan's mum got on with mine.

* * *

Back downstairs, life was a bit frosty with Mum after our earlier outburst – but not nearly as bad as it could have been. I told Mum about telling Dan, and that his mum would be expecting her to call. She said she'd do it the next night. I was dreading it.

Next day at school, I told the girls all about what had happened. As you can imagine, their comments ranged from 'You must be mad!' to 'How incredibly romantic – it's just like Meg Ryan in the movie!' Fortunately, they were equally keen to hear more about Debs's choirboy as they called him, so I was happy to let her take over and leave me space to think.

Good grief, this boyfriend business was hard work. They certainly don't tell you that it's like this in the magazines, do they?

From: sam@newshoes.com
To: butter@friedeggs.com
claudia@raginglooney.co.uk
debs@doobopdaloola.com

My mum spoke to Dan's mum and we're going to meet up the weekend after next! But our mums are coming with us! :-}! Help!

From: claudia@raginglooney.co.uk
To: sam@newshoes.com

Dead romantic. Let me know if he's got any good-looking mates!

From: butter@friedeggs.com
To: sam@newshoes.com

Supposing he turns out to be a geek? He might be shorter than u!

From: sam@newshoes.com
To: debs@doobopdaloola.com

Debs - supposing he's shorter than me? Disaster!

From: debs@doobopdaloola.com
To: sam@newshoes.com

So what if he is? Just go and have a great time!

From: danjbrown@sooper.net
To: sam@newshoes.com

My mum really liked yours. And I'm really
looking forward to meeting u.

From: sam@newshoes.com
To: danjbrown@sooper.net

Me too. But I'm five foot ten. ru shorter
than me?

From: danjbrown@sooper.net
To: sam@newshoes.com

Actually I'm five foot eight.

Joke! Dan

So how tall was he?

Chapter 8

:-)
(Happy)

The next couple of weeks flashed by in a whirl of school-work, e-mails, chats and text messages. There was never a day that went by without Dan and me speaking or at least communicating in some way. He always had some story to tell about sick animals – he really was into this vet thing. And he sometimes moaned about his little brother Tom. I've often fancied having a brother or sister so I couldn't appreciate what Dan was on about. Except there were quite a few times when Dan and I were speaking on the phone and Tom would start to pester Dan. One of those times, Dan just rang off and I was left on the other end wondering what on earth was going on. I was like, 'hello?' But then Dan rang back and explained that Tom had really excelled himself in the irritating department – and had cut him off!

'I told you I needed rescuing from my brother,' Dan laughed.

Dan always made me laugh. He made me feel good and

that made me want to meet him all the more. Even though Mum and Dad had given me quite a hard time at first it was all planned. I was to go with Mum in the car to this shopping centre. Fortunately Dad was on a business trip, otherwise I suppose he would have had to come too, to hold his little girl's hand! We were going to meet in the Pizza Place just before lunch-time and take it from there. I can't tell you how nervous I was! It was bad enough to meet Dan for the first time but to have his mum and my mum there as well was just awful! Dead embarrassing.

The girls helped me work out what to wear (very *She's Gotta Have It*) and I ended up borrowing something from all of them. And we practised all these conversations in case there were any bad moments: like if he told me I'd got spinach stuck on my teeth or if I dropped my cup of coffee all over him. But none of us could think up a really good excuse as to what to do if he turned out to be a geek – although I was sure there wasn't much chance of that because he seemed so nice on the phone.

The night before we drove up there I thought I'd never get to sleep, I was so nervous. Fortunately, I didn't wake up with bags under my eyes or a spot on my chin. But I did wake up to this e-mail:

From: danjbrown@sooper.net
To: sam@newshoes.com

Looking forward to seeing u. Hope my
hunchback doesn't put u off. At least u'll
be able to recognise me!

I hoped he was as much fun to be with as his e-mails, and
he wasn't something straight from central casting . . .

I guessed who Dan was as soon as we walked into the Pizza
Place. He was wearing a Tommy Hilfiger jacket and had thick
brown hair. He was kind of cute to look at too. Not in a
Peter Pan way though. Just kind of – well, nice, for want of a
better word. You know what I mean – not drop-dead
gorgeous – in fact, not dissimilar to Tom Hanks. Spooky!

His mum smiled at us and stood up from the table. 'Mrs
McArthur? I'm Sandra Brown.' They shook hands.

'Oh, please call me Laura. It's good to meet you.'

'Hi, Sam.' Dan stood up. That was when I realised that he
was so tall. He was well over six feet! What a relief!

'Hi.' I tried to smile but I suddenly came over all self-
conscious.

Mrs Brown called the waitress and ordered some coffee
for all of us. Then we sat and chatted about our respective
journeys there and the weather. All that kind of stuff. It was
weird. It was when Dan's mum and mine started talking
about schools that Dan caught my eye and winked at me. I
smiled back and he winked again. When were these two

going to go? Were they for real?

We'd probably been sitting talking for half an hour when Mum and Mrs Brown suddenly seemed to remember why we were there. At least they seemed to get on well! They made some excuses about going off to do some shopping.

'So, we'll meet you both back here in a couple of hours' time, then?' Mrs Brown smiled.

'Sure!' Dan and I both said at the same time. And we watched them head off into the crowd outside.

'I thought they'd never go!' Dan smiled at me. 'So, Sam, it's good to meet at last. How are you doing?'

After that, Dan and I chatted away like crazy. I didn't have to use any of the practice conversations at all. Dan was so easy to talk to – a real laugh. I told him all about the girls and we talked about his friends and what his house was like. It sounded really cosy. You know, coming home to a house full of people and animals every day. Not at all like my house – not that I'm complaining though. It just sounded different.

The waitress came over and asked if we wanted any more to eat.

'Oh, about half a ton of ice cream each, please!' Even the waitress laughed at Dan's joke. I was glad that I didn't have to worry about being with a boy who ate less than I did! In fact, Dan ate even more than me – perhaps it was because he had such long legs that needed filling up with food!

We talked about the tennis camp as we ate our ice cream.

'Is there anyone else coming from your club, then?' Dan asked.

'No, don't think so. How about yours?'

'Oh, this girl Sally that I play mixed doubles with. No one else.'

A girl? I hadn't thought about Dan having girls as friends as well as boys. I mean, me and my friends can't even rustle up one boy between us.

'Anyway,' Dan had finished his ice cream and looked at his watch, 'they're going to be back soon, aren't they?'

'Yes.' I know it sounds corny but I really didn't want the afternoon to end.

'I'm really pleased you could come, Sam.'

'So am I. It was good to meet you.'

'It won't be long before tennis camp though. Only about another six weeks.'

Six weeks! That was ages away!

Dan leaned over the table towards me. He had his arms on the table and, I couldn't swear it, but I really think he was going to touch my hand. But just then our mums arrived.

'Hello again, you two,' Mum said as they both sat down, laden with shopping bags. I don't know which of them had the most.

'Had a good time, then?' said Mrs Brown. 'Oh, can you get us both a cup of tea, love?'

So Dan ordered them their tea and that was the end of our First Date.

On the way home Mum interrogated me about Dan. I told her bits and pieces about what we had talked about. To be honest, I was so happy about how well the whole thing had gone that I didn't really mind telling her all the stuff that Dan had told me about his life and his family. He was good news and good news is always worth telling.

It didn't take too long to get home and then we had the fun of opening all the carrier bags of things that Mum had bought. It was mostly clothes for her and Dad but she had bought me a really ace jacket – it was just like one I'd told her about seeing in a catalogue. My mum can be pretty cool.

As soon as I could I went upstairs to send an e-mail to Dan. I wanted to e-mail him first. But when I got there I was too late:

From: danjbrown@sooper.net
To: sam@newshoes.com

Did I mention you were pretty too? Can't wait for tennis camp.

Charly was curled up on my bed and she cocked her ear up when she heard me gasp 'Oh wow!' when I read that. I rushed over to her and gave her a cuddle. 'Charly, you are gorgeous!'

Before I went to bed that night, I worked out what to e-mail in reply to Dan.

From: sam@newshoes.com
To: danjbrown@sooper.net

You're not so bad yourself.

On Sunday morning, there were messages from all the girls:

From: debs@doobopdaloola.com
To: sam@newshoes.com

Was he gorgeous? Gross? Call me!

From: butter@friedeggs.com
To: sam@newshoes.com

Hope you weren't disappointed. What's he like? Reveal all!

From: claudia@raginglooney.co.uk
To: sam@newshoes.com

Has he got spots? Is he nice?

So I e-mailed them all back with the same message:

He's cute. Not short – over six feet! Not a
geek but really smart. No zits. You'd really
like him. But u can't have him because he's
mine! Tell u more at school.

That night, Dan rang me on my mobile while I was working in my room.

'Hi, Sam. How are you?'

'Fine, thanks. You?' I was a bit nervous. I mean, supposing the meeting the day before had been a bit of a dream? Or perhaps he'd regretted sending me that message?

'Great. I told my mate Will all about you. He's dead jealous and says do you have any friends like you?'

Did I have any friends!

'Actually I've got three and they are all great! Anyway, I told you all about them yesterday. Maybe I should persuade them all to come on tennis camp.'

'No way – I want you to myself. I don't want all your friends there to take you away from me.'

Talking to Dan wasn't a struggle at all. I had nothing to

worry about since yesterday. Nothing to worry about at all, because an hour later, we reluctantly agreed that we had to go and get on with some work.

From: danjbrown@sooper.net
To: sam@newshoes.com

Can't believe it's a whole week since we met! Where have u been all my life? Twisted my arm playing tennis today. It hurts and I want u to rub it better! :-(

From: sam@newshoes.com
To: danjbrown@sooper.net

Does this mean u won't be able to play? Hope u get better soon. Got to spend time practising piano tonight. I've got a new piece to get to grips with for my exam. :-)

'Hi, Sam. Thought I'd call you! How are you?'

'Fine, thanks. How's your arm? Can you play?'

'Oh sure – it won't stop me from going to camp, don't worry. Only four weeks to go!'

We caught up on each other's news and then Dan told me that he's got a summer job working at a dog kennels, of all places.

'That's really good,' I said.

'Yes, I'll be able to catch up with my howling, won't I?'

We laughed. Dan often still joked about being a werewolf in disguise. 'Listen,' he said, 'I've got to go.'

'OK then. Bye, Dan.'

'Bye, Sam. Take care.'

I told the girls every day about my chats and e-mails with Dan. They always wanted to find out more and were really keen to see what he looked like. I promised I'd take my camera to tennis camp and let them see how nice he was in the flesh. The last few weeks of school passed by in a rush of school trips, homework plans for the holidays, reading lists and all that sort of stuff. Butter was finally selected for the national girls' cricket team and we used it as an excuse to go out and celebrate with a slap-up meal at Claudia's restaurant.

Dan and I spoke to each other as often as we could. When we couldn't, we caught up with each other with e-mails and he sent these really funny text messages to me – you know, the ones that look like pictures when you turn them sideways?

Suddenly, there was only a week to go before Dan and I were to meet again. The tennis camp started two days after term ended, although Dan was going to have had a whole week off school beforehand. In between the school concert (I had to play one of my 'party pieces' as Dad calls them), and scrabbling to get work handed in on time, I got together my kit for tennis camp. Over the next week, and after much discussion and debate, the girls came over and lent me some of their clothes again. I was prepared for just about every social occasion going except for skiing! Mum was really cool and bought me a new tennis racket so that I could take two with me. Dad even lent me his laptop so that I could e-mail home.

Before I knew it, it was the night before my journey to camp. Mum and Dad were going to drive me up there. I spent the evening packing, unpacking, and packing again. I spoke to all of the girls on the phone – I think they were as excited about it as me. It was odd though, because I didn't hear from Dan.

I went over to check that everything was in order on my PC before I went to bed. There was an e-mail from Dan:

From: danjbrown@sooper.net
To: sam@newshoes.com

Can't get thru on the phone. All u do is
chat to your mates! Can't wait 2cu 2morrow.
I'm the tall one with the brown hair. I
think you are the pretty one with long dark
hair. Spot you there! :-) xx

Chapter 9

X
(Kiss)

From: sam@newshoes.com

To: butter@friedeggs.com

  claudia@raginglooney.co.uk

  debs@doobopdaloola.com

Cool or what! Thought I'd have to share a
room but I've got one to myself. If this is
what university life on campus is like, I'm
coming here! There's a huge swimming pool, a
gym with the latest equipment and a kind of
common room as well. We've got a timetable
of coaching but we get some time off every
day to go out on trips. We're going to get
taken on a bus and then it's up to us what
we get up to until it's time to come back to
camp. Seen Dan! It's just as good as it was
before. No probs there. There's a really fit
coach too! He played at Wimbledon a couple

of years ago. So there's all types of
talent! Catch up with you all in a couple of
days.

On the first night, after supper, Dan and I went for a walk
around the campus.

'I can't believe we're here together, Sam.'

'It's good, isn't it? I was worried in case you'd change your
mind and not come.' And not want to see me, I thought. But
I didn't say it.

'Two whole weeks of seeing you. It's good news, I reckon.'
Dan linked his arm through mine. It felt good. Better than
anything I'd ever imagined in fact.

It was a warm and balmy night. It had been a hot summer
so far and it looked as though our two weeks would stay
that way. I just hoped that things with Dan would stay hot
too.

The coaches on the tennis camp didn't take any prisoners.
They expected us to work hard and we did, because they
made it fun as well. Dan was a good player but he wasn't as
good at singles as he was at mixed doubles. Sally, the girl he'd
mentioned before, was at camp too. During training sessions
on the first couple of days she chatted away to Dan in a
really relaxed way. She obviously really liked him. OK, so I

admit it – I was jealous of her. Not only did she and Dan get on well but they came from the same tennis club which meant that they obviously lived near one another. And Sally was better at tennis than me, too. I would have to watch out for her because she could turn out to be competition in more ways than one!

On the morning of the third day, I switched on the laptop and found mail.

From: debs@doobopdaloola.com
To: sam@newshoes.com

Is it good there? It is here – I'm meeting my choirboy again tonight.

From: claudia@raginglooney.co.uk
To: sam@newshoes.com

Have u x yet?

From: butter@friedeggs.com
To: sam@newshoes.com

Glad you're having a good time. Do all the boys have rippling muscles, then?

I did a universal e-mail back again:

All this tennis is wearing me out! Dan is
really good at it so I have to work hard to
keep up. We went to look round the city
today. We had three hours to be tourists.
I went with Dan to the cathedral and then
we looked round some shops and visited the
Roman museum. He's a really good laugh.
We've got a quiz night tonight. How's your
choirboy, Debs? Speak soon.

We split up into two teams for the quiz: girls against boys.
Naturally the girls won but it was close. I was impressed by
how much Dan knew. And not so impressed to discover
that Sally was a real brainbox. I began to dislike her more
and more as the evening progressed. Especially when she
corrected me in front of everyone when I tried to answer a
music question. I was bristling. When I mentioned it to Dan
afterwards, he didn't seem to know what I was talking about.
'Sally's not like that,' he said. But then she probably wouldn't
be with him, would she?

After the quiz, because it was so hot, Dan and I went for
a walk around the campus. There was a big pond on the
other side of the parkland and we headed for there, to sit
down on a bench overlooking the water. It looked beautiful,

with the moon sending beams reflecting off the water. Any thoughts of Sally were washed away.

'This is the life, eh, Sam?' Dan put his arm round me and I snuggled in. Fortunately, after all those years of worrying about it, being with a boy like that just comes naturally. Believe me.

'It's certainly been good so far, hasn't it? Mind you, it is only day two. Perhaps tomorrow we'll be expected to go on an army assault course to check on our stamina. I'm not so sure that I'd like that!'

'Nor me! Sam?'

'Yes?' I turned and looked up at Dan.

He looked down his gorgeous face at me. He said nothing for a moment and then leaned down towards me and put his hand on my chin. That was when he kissed me for the first time.

From: sam@newshoes.com
To: claudia@raginglooney.co.uk

Claudia – have now!

After that night, Dan and I went for a walk every night and spent time on our own. The guys that ran the camp were really cool about what we all got up to. They said it was up to us to be responsible for our own safety and that, as long as we turned up to breakfast each morning and coaching on time, and didn't disgrace the camp at anything, they'd treat us as adults. Oh, and they also said we all had to sleep in our own rooms – as if we'd do anything else anyway!

As the days passed, I wanted to spend more and more time with Dan. Don't get me wrong: I really enjoyed all the tennis. In fact, I was really improving my game. Everyone at camp seemed great. Except for Sally, who always seemed to manage to be near Dan and me at the lunch queue. And she loved getting Dan as her partner, I noticed. Other than that, camp was fab. I even remembered to e-mail Mum and Dad some nights too. Before I knew it, a whole week had passed and they gave us Sunday off.

We all went on the bus to this great place by the river. We hired boats and rowed downstream to have our picnic on the bank. We had a great day and I took loads of pictures. Bill, one of the boys, took a photo of me and Dan together. 'Got to get our very own Ross and Rachel in a picture, haven't we?' I was so embarrassed! But it's a good picture now it's been developed.

That night, I e-mailed everyone:

So cool here! I can't believe a whole week has passed. That means there's only a week left! And I don't want it to end. What have you lot been up to while I've been away? Met anyone nice? Apart from Debs's choirboy, of course.

From: butter@friedeggs.com
To: sam@newshoes.com

Sounds like you're having a great time. You managing to get any tennis in, in between snogs? The most exciting thing that's happened to me is that my cousin's staying and he's turned into a bit of a dish. But then he is my cousin . . . cu soon. x

From: claudia@raginglooney.co.uk
To: sam@newshoes.com

So he's still all right after a week, is he? When are we going to meet him? cu at the weekend. x

From: debs@doobopdaloola.com
To: sam@newshoes.com

My choirboy is not bad at all. His name is Greg. You might get to see him when you come home. cu X>X>!

The next week passed by even quicker than the first one. We had a kind of mini-tournament over the last week. Of course I didn't win but I got into the quarter-finals of my set. By the last Friday, Dan got into the semi-finals in the mixed doubles. The problem was, he played with Sally and they looked like they might even win at one point. I felt sick. I mean, I wanted Dan to win – but certainly not with Sally. I really started to hate her in those last few minutes of the game. When they lost, she ruffled Dan's hair! And I'm like, 'hello?' Who does she think she is? Dan laughed as well! Like he kind of enjoyed it. Afterwards I was really peeved with them both: surely Sally should be keeping her hands to herself? It was obvious that Dan was my boyfriend. And shouldn't Dan have made that clear to her? I was so angry that I found it really hard to commiserate with them when they lost. In fact, I skipped tea and went straight up to the girls' bathroom and had a shower before going to my room. I lay on my bed wishing that Charly could have been there to make me feel better.

It must have been about an hour later when Dan came and knocked at my door.

'Sam? You there? It's me, Dan. Sam?'

At first I didn't say anything. But he kept on knocking and in the end I opened the door and made some pathetic excuse about not hearing him. I could tell Dan didn't believe me.

'Something wrong, Sam?'

Oh, so he had noticed? 'No, I'm fine,' I said, not sounding anything like it.

'Fancy a walk before supper? Or a swim?'

'Not sure,' I said.

In the end, Dan gave up trying to cajole me into doing something with him and said he'd see me at supper in the dining-hall.

I stayed in my room on my own feeling completely miserable. How could I have been so stupid? I only had two more nights with Dan before we'd have to go home. And now I'd wasted one of them and probably made Dan go right off me anyway.

Dan was already in the dining-hall when I got there. He looked up and smiled at me, pointing to the seat next to him that he'd saved for me. There were six of us on the table and we all chatted away like we had done every night. I tried to behave like my usual cheerful self but I kept noticing Dan giving me sideways looks every now and then. Afterwards, we had another one of our quiz nights and played the 'Who Wants to be a Millionaire' board game. One of the girls got as far as £250,000!

When everything was packed up, Dan asked me if I wanted to walk with him and I said yes straight away. As we strolled around the campus, Dan asked me what earlier had been all about. God, I'd been such a geek! Like the fool I was I blurted out the truth about how I felt about Sally and ended up saying, 'I didn't know that you already had another girlfriend.'

'Sam, you idiot! Sally's not my girlfriend! I've known her since we were at primary school together. She's just a friend. You're my girlfriend, Sam. And I've never had a girlfriend like you before. Do you forgive me for whatever it is you think I've done?'

He drew me closer to him and looked down at me with his gorgeous brown eyes.

'Yes.' I couldn't say anything else. 'Sorry, I think I've been stupid.'

'You've certainly been a bit dumb, Sam. But that doesn't matter, because I think I love you.'

I promise you that was actually what he said! We spent the rest of the night hugging each other and kissing.

Dan and I spent the last day at camp as inseparables. We sat next to each other to watch the mixed doubles finals and then we had the joy of watching Sally lose in the girls' singles for her set. OK, so it's bitchy of me to be glad that she lost. But whatever Dan said, I still didn't trust her as far as my boyfriend was concerned. After that, we went on the camp trip together. We didn't bother to team up with any of the others because, without saying anything to each other, we both seemed to realise that we just had to spend the time on our own because who knew when we were going to see each other again.

After supper that night, we went for our usual walk.

'Dan, I really don't want to go home tomorrow.'

'Me neither. I can't bear the thought of not seeing you after tomorrow morning.'

We sat down on the bench by the lake and put our arms round each other.

'Sam, I've been thinking. Do you think perhaps you could come and see me at my house? I mean, once I've gone back I've got to do my job at the kennels so I won't get any more time off. But I thought perhaps you could come up and stay for a week? I'm not sure when. What do you think?'

'I'd love to.' I hugged him tighter. It felt good that he wanted me to go to meet his family properly. And his friends. But then I remembered the real world outside the tennis camp. 'But I'll have to check it out with my parents first.'

'Course.' Dan smiled at me.

We spent the rest of the evening on that bench, not really wanting to think about the next morning.

* * *

We said our farewells by the bench the next morning after breakfast. My parents came to get me soon after that. I said goodbye to everyone except Dan. He stood at the back of the crowded hallway as if he was trying to blend into the paintwork. But then my der-brained Dad insisted he 'had to meet this young man Dan that I spent so much time talking to!' He obviously thought he was dead witty. I wanted to die – it was like he was suddenly a few tennis balls short of a game instead of his normal human-being self! So there was this cringe-making ten minutes when Dan had to make small talk to my dad – thank God his mum and dad weren't there as well or they all might have suggested we had tea and cucumber sandwiches together when all Dan and I wanted to do was be on our own. In the end, I think Mum realised and suggested that she and Dad went and put my bag in the car. Dan and I just stood there looking at each other, oblivious to all the other kids. Dan put his arms round me one more time.

'Bye, Sam. It's been great.'

'Yes.' I just couldn't say anything else. But as I turned back to swing my rucksack over my shoulder I caught his eye. I'm sure he was crying but before I could tell for sure, he turned and walked away.

Despite everything it was still good to see my parents. They wanted to know all about the camp on the journey home and I told them quite a lot before I couldn't bear to speak any longer. It was as if the further away I got from Dan the sadder I felt. So I made some excuse about being tired because there had been a really late party the night before. Dad gave me a weird look. But I think Mum had an idea of how I felt because she leaned back and squeezed my hand without saying anything.

I pretended to sleep in the back seat and sneaked my mobile out of my bag to send Dan a message. He'd already sent me one:

Luv u. x

Chapter 10

thx a lot!
(Thanks a lot!)

Coming home was awful. I mean, it was good to see Mum and Dad, of course, and great to see Charly again and all of the girls. But — and it was a big but — I couldn't see Dan, could I? It was like Depression City being without him. Sure I could speak to him on the phone (and we did, frequently) and e-mail him (sometimes two or three a day) but I couldn't see him or touch him and just be with him.

I moped about for quite a bit and everyone got fed up with me.

'For goodness sake, Sam! Get a life! OK, so Dan's great and all that but he's only a boy!' Butter said.

Only a boy! Well, it was obvious that no one as special as Dan had walked into her life, wasn't it? Even so, after a week or so, I realised that the girls did have a point. There wasn't much I could do about it, what with Dan being so far away. And it had turned out that for various reasons to do with Dan's family coming to stay, I wasn't going to be able to go up to his for some time. But at least my mum and dad had agreed to Dan coming to stay for the weekend. He was coming halfway through the summer holidays for the bank holiday weekend and that was when I was going to get the chance to introduce Dan to all the girls. Then they'd know why I'd been missing him so much.

In the meantime, I had to keep myself occupied by playing more tennis with the girls (Butter was quite good but she did go off to a cricket training camp so I lost her as a tennis partner for a while), swimming (we all went together), playing the piano, and generally mooching around the house and garden with Charly. The days were long ones because of Mum and Dad being out at work so much but a couple of days a week Mum insisted that Rose, the lady who helps to clean our house, spent most of the day with me. Rose is really sweet — I've known her for ever — but she made me feel like I was still a kid. She even made me banana milkshakes, if you please! Still, at least my parents said it was OK for the girls to come over now and then to spend the day. And I also had my e-mails to and from Dan to look forward to as well as talking to him on the phone. But it was difficult for Dan to speak to me that often because he was so busy with his work at the kennels. Still, he always e-mailed me or sent me a text message if he couldn't ring.

```
From: danjbrown@sooper.net
To: sam@newshoes.com
Hi! Can't wait 2 cu at the station tomorrow!
Don't be late. Luv Dan x @>—>—
```

The day arrived at last! I left home early to meet Dan at the station because I had to get a bus before I got on the tube which then got me to the station. As I result, I arrived so early at the mainline station that I had to hang around waiting for Dan. I must have had to wait for about an hour before his train eventually chugged its way to the platform. I leaped to the barrier and looked anxiously for Dan. People were pouring off the train and I couldn't see Dan amongst them. Perhaps he hadn't caught the train? Perhaps he'd changed his mind! Perhaps he'd tried to phone me? I fished my phone out of my pocket to check it. It was switched on like I thought. I hadn't had any messages. So where was he?

'Well, hi there! Meeting someone by any chance?'

I almost jumped out of my skin! Of course it was Dan. He was standing right next to me, grinning from ear to ear. We kind of fell into each other's arms and stood there hugging each other. It felt good until the ticket collector said, 'Excuse me, you two, but do you think you could move along and let the passengers get on their train?' which was pretty embarrassing.

I took Dan back to my house and he seemed to be amazed by my knowledge of the Underground system and the buses – he really was a novice about being in London and I was glad that, even though I was two years younger, I was able to take charge.

Back home, we had some lunch and then we went off to meet up with the girls at the park café. Suddenly I was feeling nervous about it.

From: butter@friedeggs.com

To: sam@newshoes.com

Not bad! I suppose u want to keep him to yourself for the rest of the wknd! Have a great one. Luvya!

From: debs@doobopdaloola.com

To: sam@newshoes.com

Furious u found him on the net and I didn't! Spk soon. Luv!

From: claudia@raginglooney.co.uk

To: sam@newshoes.com

What a hunk! Don't do anything I wouldn't do! xx

So I needn't have worried about it. As you can see, Dan charmed the pants off them. Not that he had to do it in an oily way. No, he just did it by being himself. The rest of the weekend went so quickly it was over in a flash. It wasn't nearly as awkward as I thought it would be, mostly because my parents weren't really around that much. Definitely one of the benefits of being an only child with parents who work so hard: they give you your space. On the Saturday night we all went to the health club for the summer barbecue and because there were so many people there, Dan and I managed to just hang out together. We even had a boogie along with the jazz band that was playing. On the Sunday, Mum and Dad went to visit some friends so Dan and I went for a picnic along the river and watched all the rowing crews practising.

Then it was Monday and Dan and I were making our way back on the Underground to the station. We hugged each other for as long as possible until Dan simply had to get on the train before they shut the barrier. It was really hard not to cry.

On the bus home I got a text message:

```
had no plans
for half term.
have now!
chat 8.
```

At eight that night, when we did chat, Dan asked me to go up to his place for half term! At least it was something to look forward to. But it was ages away!

The rest of the summer was a bit grim! Sure the sun shone and the nights were long – but that only seemed to emphasise that there was no point in any of it if Dan wasn't around. Dan and I spoke frequently and exchanged messages all the time. But it's not the same as being with each other. Debs was having a great time with her choirboy and then, to crown it all, when we went back to school, Butter announced that she was seeing some boy she'd met at the cricket nets and Claudia had the hots for someone who was working at her parents' restaurant.

I tried to put a braver face on it. After all Dan and I did have something special: we had each other. Even if there was two hundred miles between us.

As we approached our exams, we seemed to get more and more coursework and endless lists of books from all our teachers that they reckoned we needed to read because they were essential to passing our exams. On top of that I was working towards my next piano exam. Some nights it wasn't until bedtime that I managed to find time to respond to Dan's e-mails. But then I also noticed that, whereas before Dan always used to contact me somehow as soon as he came home, he often didn't manage to have time to get in touch with me until later. Of course, he had his A level mocks coming up.

Fortunately, half term did eventually arrive – along with the darker winter nights and the chilly air. I made the journey to the station and set off to Dan's house for the week.

On the way there my phone rang.

'Hello?'

'Sam! How are you doing?' It was Dan!

'Fine! Where are you?'

'On my way to the station to meet you. I've borrowed Dad's Land Rover. See you in about twenty minutes.'

And he hung up.

Twenty-five minutes later we were in each other's arms.

It was fantastic being with Dan again. His mum made me feel really welcome: she'd baked all these cakes and when I arrived we had tea in the kitchen which had a roaring log fire over at one end. It wasn't a bit like our house. There was a heap of dogs in the corner next to the stove and every time someone came into the kitchen they went bonkers, jumping up at people. They weren't a bit like my sleek Charly and every time I saw the dogs I remembered her and missed her. Don't get me wrong – it was great being with Dan but it did remind me of what I had at home too. Being a vet, Dan's dad seemed to be in and out of the house at really peculiar times. In at the sort of times my mum and dad would never be at home and then, suddenly, the phone might go in the middle of the evening meal and his dad would have to rush off to look after a sick horse or a cow that was about to give birth to a calf that had got stuck. Gross or what?

It was dead embarrassing because the first time I went with Dan on a farm visit I had to borrow Mrs Brown's wellies and I had to cram my feet into them because she's much shorter and smaller than me. Even worse, I was wearing this really great pair of bootlegs that were embroidered with sequins and beads. It was almost impossible to cram those in the wellies. And the farmer couldn't resist going on and on about how he'd never had anyone so well-dressed in his sheep shed before. He thought it was hysterical, you could tell. Dan kind of laughed with him. Then I tripped in the mud and got it, and who knows what else, all over my hands and arms. I was not enjoying myself. But I could tell Dan just loved being there amongst all that gunk. He leaped out of his mum's car and was right in there, helping with the sheep straight away. I was glad to be with Dan but, quite frankly, I couldn't really see why sticking jabs into sheep was quite as exciting as Dan found it.

'Something wrong, Sam?' Dan asked, glancing up at me, as

he had his hand in a position which looked suspiciously close to a sheep's bottom.

'Oh, nothing. I'm having a great time,' I lied, pulling my jacket closer to me in an attempt to keep warm in the howling gale that was brewing up around the barn.

Afterwards, I sulked in the car.

'Is there a problem, Sam? You don't seem all that happy,' Dan said.

'I just thought that the whole point of me coming up here was so that we could spend some time together.' I'd said it now.

'But we are, Sam.' Dan didn't get it.

'Yes – but surrounded by cow muck and smelly animals! We're never on our own – there's always some animal or your brother around!'

Dan just gawped at me and obviously didn't know what to say. I sat there in silence as Dan drove the car. Then suddenly he blurted out, 'But I thought you'd want to join in with all the things I enjoy! You know, see why I really want to be a vet!'

'And I thought I'd come up here because you wanted to see me.'

We sat in silence until we got back to his house. Dan switched off the engine and looked at me. I started to cry and Dan put his arms round me. We ended up both apologising at once. It cleared the air (except, of course, for the smelly wellies steaming away in the back of the car) and Dan said, 'OK, no more sheep or cows while you're here.'

'Good,' I said, and we kissed and made up properly.

But even that wasn't the end of our problems. Dan's brother Tom had started off by being quite cute, but he ended up being a total pain. Like I say, at first it was quite good fun to have Tom around. He made us cups of coffee and seemed to want to know all about me and London. But then it got to the point that every time Dan and I were alone in the living-room or the kitchen, Tom came in and tried to tell stupid jokes or made slurping and sucking noises as if he was snogging with a cushion. It was embarrassing and boring and Dan really lost his rag with him a couple of times. But it didn't seem to stop Tom. He was a nightmare! Thank goodness I haven't got someone like him at home!

On the Friday, Dan and I went to a barn dance to meet up with all his friends. They were really friendly. It was good, although they did keep asking me questions about London. They seemed to think that it was a really dangerous place with drug dealers hanging around on every street corner and old ladies being mugged at the bus stop all the time. The barn dance was really good fun and everyone I met was really nice. But they were all so different from the girls. I don't quite know how exactly. But they were. Perhaps it was because they seemed to spend so much time doing things with their families. I mean, they'd all known each other for ever. They all knew each other's parents, and some of them were even related to each other. They'd all been to the same schools for ever and they all seemed to behave as if they'd never not known each other. Back home, I hardly knew some of my friends' parents. Debs was a bit different, I admit. I mean, I'd slept over at hers a few times and once at Claudia's. But I still didn't really know my mates' parents like Dan's friends did. My life at school and my life at home were two entirely separate universes.

Saturday night, we all trekked to the nearest town and went for a pizza and then to the cinema and that was when I began to realise quite how well they all did know each other. Sally was there. It seemed that Dan didn't just spend time with Sally at tennis club. In fact, I began to wonder if Sally and Dan had once been an item. Or if maybe she fancied him becoming one, once I'd got back to London . . .

Chapter 11

just gr8!
(Just great!)

Dan and I had a couple of hours to ourselves the morning of my last day there. His mum and dad went off to church with Tom and left us, wishing me a good journey home and saying that they hoped I'd come and stay again soon.

After they'd gone, Dan and I had a last cup of coffee together in the kitchen.

'Do you reckon that we will be able to have some time together during the Christmas holidays?' I asked.

'Don't know, Sam.' Dan held my hand across the table. 'You know what Christmas is like, with all the family getting together and that.'

I didn't, because my mum and dad were only children and my gran and grandad on my dad's side had died when I was a baby. My other gran and grandad always went on a cruise for Christmas. They were cool.

'Sure,' I said, not meaning it at all.

'Then of course there are the exams coming up,' Dan

went on. 'I've had an offer to go and see one of the universities I've applied for just before Christmas.'

This was the first time he'd mentioned it to me. I tried not to sound surprised but, rather irritatingly, I don't think it worked.

'Oh, where's that, then?' I was desperately hoping it would be London, or at least closer to London. Do vets study to be vets in London?

'St Andrews. In Scotland.'

'Scotland?' I wasn't even trying to pretend not to be surprised now. 'But that's miles away. That's . . .' I spluttered, 'another country.' I looked at Dan. Surely he'd want to move closer to me, not further away?

'Well, yes, it is. And it's also a really great university with loads going on. And it's a good vet school. Sam? What's the problem?'

What's the problem? Was he living on another planet?

'Nothing,' I lied, holding back the tears. I didn't want to ruin our last moments together. Especially as it was obviously going to be some time next year that we saw each other again.

He carried on holding my hand which made me feel better. 'It's been great having you here this week,' he said, 'before all the really hard work starts. I've really got to put the work in to get some decent grades in the exams. How about you?'

'Sure, yes,' I smiled. Of course I was going to work hard but studying wasn't going to completely take over my life, was it?

Soon after that, we left for the station. We didn't say much in the car and stood holding hands at the station platform.

Once I was on the train, I sent Dan a message:

```
gr8 time.
thx. luv u
```

I waited to see if I got a message back. He obviously had his phone switched off.

Mum and Dad came to meet me at the station in London. They asked me all about my week and I told them the important bits. But then I made the excuse of feeling tired and went up to my room.

It was great to see Charly again and I had a whole load of e-mails from the girls when I got back. There was one from Dan as well:

```
From: danjbrown@sooper.net
To: sam@newshoes.com
Can't ring 2nite. Hope u had a good journey.
Speak l8tr in the week.
```

Not what I was expecting at all. So I went to bed that night and had a good old cry.

The second half of term was, like Dan had said it would be, hard work. The teachers seemed to put us all into overdrive and we had to work hard towards our mocks. Thank goodness most of our exam results came from coursework though! Dan obviously meant exactly what he said about his studies though. We chatted far less often in the week and it nearly always seemed to be me that e-mailed or messaged him first. Still, he always sent cheery messages back. When he got round to sending them, that is.

My piano exam came and went. Dan sent me a really sweet card wishing me luck! Debs was still having her fling with her choirboy and Butter was going out on and off with her boy. As for Claudia and her guy, well, as she said, it's difficult to flirt under your parents' nose when the person you are flirting with is meant to be working for them. But they all kept telling me how lucky I was to have Dan. 'Yes, he's great,' I always said, wondering how great it really was to have a boyfriend you could never actually see . . .

From: sam@newshoes.com
To: danjbrown@sooper.net

How ru getting on? Wondered if you'd changed

your mind about Christmas? Got any time
in the New Year to come down to the Big
Smoke?

XOXOX Sam

It was the end of November and it was two days before I
even heard from Dan. Then one night, thankfully when I was
working in my room, my phone went.

'Hi, Sam. How are you doing?'

'Fine thanks, you?'

'OK, working hard, you know the sort of thing.' He was
the one who had rung me but he sounded distracted, as if
he was actually doing something else. I soon found out he
was – he was keying something into his PC.

'How's the work going?' I asked cheerily, trying to make
out I didn't mind.

'OK, but there's so much of it. I went off to St Andrews
the other day.'

'How was that?' He hadn't mentioned he was going.

'Fantastic. I met some really friendly people there. It's
definitely my first choice, so now I've absolutely *got* to get
the grades.'

We carried on chatting like that for a while and then Dan
brought up the subject of my last e-mail.

'The problem is I've got so much stuff going on at the

moment. And I already told you Christmas and New Year was going to be difficult.'

'Yes, I know, I just thought I'd ask in case your plans had changed.' I tried to sound blasé about it as if I didn't mind. I was trying so hard to be cool.

'Listen, Sam, I don't want to hurt your feelings or anything. It's just that you seem to want more out of this relationship than I do. We had a really great time together but, well, I've got so much on my plate at the moment. I need my time to study. I'd really like to stay friends with you, you know?'

I was speechless. I simply didn't know what to say. I was in shock. The tears stung my eyes.

'Sam, are you OK? You're not, are you? Sam?'

Not OK? What did he think I was? I was supposed to be the person he loved and he was telling me he just wanted to be friends. OK? Not OK.

Eventually I gathered my thoughts together. 'I'm fine, thanks. Yes, you're right. I've got lots on my plate, too. Listen, I've got to go. Got some work to do. Speak to you soon.'

'Sure, yes. Sam, I'll call you later in the week, OK?'

'Bye.'

I never had that phone call.

* * *

I was numb with shock and just carried on as if nothing had changed for a week or so. I didn't even tell the girls what had happened. I mean, how could I tell them that Mr Wonderful had dumped me? Mum guessed though. She was cool about it and didn't pry or anything at first. But then one night she came into my room as I cried myself to sleep with Charly curled up at my feet.

'Samantha? Do you mind if I come in?'

I turned over to face the wall and buried myself deep into the duvet. What if she saw me crying? But she gently stroked my hair. Charly was giving a low purr of comfort at my feet.

'Oh, darling girl. I can't bear to watch you like this. Has something happened? Something with Dan?'

I didn't say anything at first. But eventually, I couldn't bottle it up any longer and I told her everything about Dan dumping me over the phone.

'Samantha, love. I could say all sorts of things – like how you'll get over it. And how he doesn't deserve someone like you. And the line about there being plenty more fish in the sea. But they won't comfort you, I know. Because I remember my mum saying all those things to me when my first boyfriend ditched me.'

Now that brought me up with a start. I mean, I suppose I never thought of my mum as ever having had any boyfriends other than Dad. In the end, Mum went down and made both of us a cup of hot chocolate and we sat together on my bed with Charly and snuggled together. I asked Mum more about the boyfriends she'd had. It turned out she'd been out with quite a lot of lads. And she was really funny about some of them, although she told me about one she'd been engaged to who'd suddenly put the whole thing off. I could tell she'd been badly hurt by it. I found out a lot about Mum that night and, although I can't pretend that I didn't hurt any more, I did feel a bit better about it. After all, I was now a fully-fledged member of the girls-dating-boys club.

It was a few days more before the girls found out. Of course, it was Debs that worked it out first. She said that she thought I was looking a bit peaky. Which was true because I never seemed to be able to get to sleep these nights. I just kept thinking of Dan. And whether he was with Sally. And the fact that he'd dumped me.

'So what's up, Sam?' Debs asked kindly at the rehearsal we had for the school concert. She and I were both playing in it and singing in the choir with all of the others.

'Just a bit fed up, that's all.'

'I know you better than that, Sam. Tell me later.'

So it was afterwards when we were walking to the bus stop that she asked me how Dan was and if I was going to see him at Christmas. I just burst into tears and told her everything. Debs whisked me off to a café, away from everyone else, and I sat there telling her over and over again what Dan had said. As if somehow, by repeating myself what he'd said, it was going to change things.

'I don't believe it! I don't!' Debs said, holding my hand, hugging me and even giving me paper napkins to blow my nose on. She was so angry about Dan on my behalf, I think she'd have slugged him one if he had happened to be anywhere near her. But then, of course, he wasn't, he was miles away. Debs suggested that it would be better if she spilt the beans to the others. I protested at first, but then I began to see the sense of getting it over with. And I knew that Debs would do it kindly.

That night, I received loads of e-mails, all sending TLC, from the girls. At first I was really embarrassed that they knew. Then, as they all showed how much they cared and I realised they weren't there to gloat and say 'told you so', I began to feel a bit better about it.

Claudia said he was an idiot and that I was too good for him. Butter agreed and said that was what he couldn't cope with.

Term carried on. And I kind of limped my way through it. I found it hard to look forward to anything. I just got up every morning and went through the motions of every day at school and homework until it was late enough for me to go to bed. Then I'd lie there with Charly curled up on my chest, unable to sleep. Mum tried to comfort me, but I think that she knew it was something I had to sort out for myself. She took me on a few shopping treats at the weekends. They were fun, but I still hurt inside. Of course, Debs was just fantastic and never mentioned her choirboy. The other girls did their best with me, too.

After a few weeks I was so exhausted by lack of sleep that I finally crashed into slumber one night. I woke up feeling dreadful, with my head pounding – I had a really bad cold. I looked really attractive, with black bags under my red eyes and a glowing sore nose.

I couldn't seem to get into the swing of the Christmas festivities like I normally would. Some days I felt defiant and that I really wanted to show Dan how I didn't need him (only I couldn't think how I was meant to). Other days I just felt like I wanted to crawl into a hole because I missed Dan and his humour (and his love) so much! But eventually, as the days went by, it did somehow get easier. I think it was when I stopped anticipating that he might surprise me and phone or e-mail.

In fact, for at least two weeks, I honestly think that I stopped even thinking about Dan. Debs persuaded me to go out with her and the girls to the cinema and we had a good laugh hanging out at a burger bar afterwards.

'Welcome back, Sam,' Claudia said just before our mums arrived to take us home that night.

'What? What do you mean?' I was surprised at what she'd said.

'You're looking much happier again, Sam. Like our old mate.'

'Isn't it great?' said Debs to the other two.

'Certainly is,' agreed Butter. 'Who needs lads?'

'Not me,' I laughed. Real mates were better any day.

But then, on the day of the concert, Dan had the nerve to send me a Christmas card. 'Hope you have a good one!' it said. Do boys have any feelings at all? I couldn't be bothered to send one back. I mean, what was I going to say to him? Was I supposed to send him all my love as if what he'd done didn't really matter at all? That was when I knew that I was over him.

Two days before the end of term, the girls were talking about the school disco. It was going to be a joint one with the local boys' school. 'You are coming, aren't you?' Butter asked.

'Not sure. I hadn't really thought about it.' It was true.

'You've got to!' Claudia said.

'Yeah, it wouldn't be the same without you,' the others said.

In the end, they bullied me into saying yes.

I had to go home to rummage in my wardrobe to find something to wear. I was looking forward to going. I was going to have fun!

On the actual night, I listened to a Britney CD while I got myself ready. It really got me in the mood. Mum drove me to the disco.

'You're looking really nice, Samantha,' Mum said, as she pulled up outside the school gates.

'Thanks, Mum,' I smiled, zipping my jacket. 'See you later.'

'You will, sweetheart. Have a great time.'

'I think I will!'

I met up with the girls in the loo so we could put on our final bits of make-up before we went in. One of the teachers from the boys' school was running the disco but actually he wasn't that bad. The four of us bopped away with the best of them and had a really good laugh. Who needs boyfriends when you've got best friends? A couple of times we did the routines that we'd memorised from some videos. Butter even did a karaoke number! This was more like Christmas fun time!

There was a group of boys dancing next to us for most of the evening. They were quite good dancers for boys and they were quite a good laugh too. We all had a good giggle about them when we trooped off to the loo.

'Don't fancy yours much,' joked Claudia as she brushed on even more mascara.

'I do!' I said and we giggled so much our sides ached.

Back in the hall, we launched ourselves at the food.

'You live near Manor Park, don't you? I've seen you on the bus.' It was one of the boys from earlier.

He had? I'd never even noticed him but he was as good-looking as the blond one in 'Hollyoaks'!

'Yes, that's right. Where d'you live, then?'

It turned out that his name was Jon and he lived about ten minutes away from me.

'Us lot are going to the concert at the Town Hall next week. Do you fancy coming?'

He was asking me to go with them and I wasn't sure what to say. 'I think your friend Butter's coming. Looks like Claudia might be too.' Jon nodded over towards them both. They were deep in conversation with two of Jon's friends. (Debs, of course, was with Greg.)

'OK, then,' I smiled. He seemed OK. And he wasn't a geek either. Or short.

We spent the rest of the disco with all of us dancing together. I really had a good time – I was smiling so much my face ached. The evening ended with a slow dance. I don't know why, but I wasn't at all embarrassed when Jon asked me to dance with him. And it was good. Fortunately, he didn't go and spoil it all by trying to grope me. But he did kiss me on the cheek when we got our coats and said goodbye. And he seemed to understand when I said my mum was meeting me outside to take me home.

We swopped phone numbers. 'I'll call you to arrange where we can meet, OK?'

'Sure. Night.' I smiled.

'Night, Sam. See you!'

From: claudia@raginglooney.co.uk
To: sam@newshoes.com

u don't hang about much, do u? Aren't they nice?

From: butter@friedeggs.com
To: sam@newshoes.com

Is yours as nice as mine?

From: sam@newshoes.com
To: butter@friedeggs.com

Think so!

From: debs@doobopdaloola.com

To: sam@newshoes.com

Way to go, Sam!

We all had a great time at the concert. Christmas came and went. The New Year dawned and I admit I half wondered if I'd hear from Dan. But I haven't heard from Dan since. I suppose that e-love was never really going to be true love. But I wonder if it would have been any different if we'd lived closer? Oh well, I'll never know. Anyway, tonight I'm off out with Jon.

Sunday 10.00 a.m.
I persuaded Jas to come to church with me to thank God for making Dad have his shoes blown off and also for giving me a Sex God as a plaything. When I got to Jas's house she was sitting on her wall in the shortest skirt known to humanity. She leapt off the wall. Her skirt was about four centimetres long. I said, "Is it a long time since you went to church,

Jas?" and she said, "Its OK, I'm wearing really big knickers."

Friday – police raid 5.00p.m.
We had the police round about Angus. They brought him back in a sack. The policeman held the sack at arm's length: "Is this your cat?" I couldn't help noticing that his trousers were shredded round the ankles.

"Hurray, she's back! Georgia, the muddle-headed, angst-ridden drama queen of ANGUS, THONGS AND FULL-FRONTAL SNOGGING reveals all again in a diary full of thrills, spills and hilarious escapades." Time Out – Kids Out

If you would like more information about
books available from Piccadilly Press and how
to order them, please contact us at:

Piccadilly Press Ltd.
5 Castle Road
London
NW1 8PR

Tel: 020 7267 4492
Fax: 020 7267 4493

Feel free to visit our website at
www.piccadillypress.co.uk